The Lawman's Unwelcome Christmas Bride

Cheryl Wright

Copyright

THE LAWMAN'S UNWELCOME CHRISTMAS BRIDE
(Unwelcome Brides Series – Book Four)

Copyright ©2024 by Cheryl Wright

Small Town Romance Publications

All rights reserved. Without limiting the rights under copyright reserved above, no part of this publication may be reproduced, stored in or introduced into a retrieval system, or transmitted, in any form, or by any means (electronic, mechanical, photocopying, recording, or otherwise) without the prior written permission of the copyright owner of this book.

This is a work of fiction. Characters, places, and incidents are a figment of the author's imagination. Any resemblance to actual events, locales, organizations or people living or dead, is totally coincidental.

- This book was written by a human and not Artificial Intelligence (A.I.).
- This book can not be used to train Artificial Intelligence (A.I.).

Dedication

To Margaret Tanner, my very dear friend and fellow author, for her enduring encouragement and friendship.

To Alan, my husband of over forty-nine years, who has been a relentless supporter of my writing and dreams for many years.

To You, my wonderful readers, who encourage me to continue writing these stories. It is such a joy knowing so many of you enjoy reading my stories as much as I love writing them for you.

Table of Contents

Copyright 2

Dedication 3

Table of Contents 4

Chapter One 6

Chapter Two 10

Chapter Three 16

Chapter Four 20

Chapter Five 26

Chapter Six 31

Chapter Seven 37

Chapter Eight 43

Chapter Nine 49

Chapter Ten 55

Chapter Eleven 60

Chapter Twelve 66

Chapter Thirteen 73

Chapter Fourteen 80

Chapter Fifteen 86

Chapter Sixteen 92

Chapter Seventeen 98

Chapter Eighteen	104
Chapter Nineteen	109
Chapter Twenty	115
Chapter Twenty-One	120
Chapter Twenty-Two	127
Epilogue	134
From the Author	137
About the Author	138
Links	139

Chapter One

Early December, Halliwell Junction, Montana – 1880's

Sheriff Wyatt Hawkins cast an eye across the main street of town. Nothing much was going on, which was exactly the way he liked it. He heard the train before he saw it, and hurried toward the train station.

Ever since the railway had come to town, trouble followed. With almost every stop the railway made to Halliwell Junction, havoc prevailed. They'd had their townsfolk attacked, stores rummaged, and ladies accosted by brutes of the worst kind.

If he could turn back time, Wyatt would surely make an effort to stop the railway settling in Halliwell Junction. He'd appealed to the mayor, who was having none of it.

"It will be a boon for the town," the mayor declared to anyone who would listen. As it turned out, it was a boon for criminals and the saloon that appeared shortly before the railway did.

Each and every time the train arrived, the jail cells were quickly filled. It was getting to the point where they may have to expand them.

Sheriff Hawkins shook his head. What would he be dealing with this time? Instead of pondering the negatives, he headed for the railway platform. The train whistle blew, and he quickened his steps.

It was then he saw it. Something fell off the moving train. *Was that a...woman?* His heart pounded as Wyatt headed in the direction of where he'd seen the movement. Thankfully, it happened not far before the platform when the train was traveling slowly, otherwise, she would have sustained severe injuries.

He stood at the place Wyatt believed he had seen her fall. He glanced about but saw nothing. No one. Surely his imagination wasn't playing tricks on him? He didn't need a distraction like this. Wyatt shrugged his shoulders and headed to the platform – his original destination.

The platform was all hustle and bustle, as it often was when the train arrived from Helena.

Halliwell Junction was nothing more than a small dot on a large map. Food shopping here was sketchy at best. Clothing shopping here was not what the ladies wanted.

The mercantile owners did their best to bring in gowns, nightgowns and unmentionables they believed suitable, but it was never enough. According to some husbands in town, their wives complained the variety was poor.

As a result, they would get together and go to one of the bigger towns, or even Helena, to do their clothing shopping. The range there was far more than they would ever find in Halliwell Junction.

Many had welcomed the railway with open arms. For Wyatt, it would never be a good thing. He knew the evil that found its way to town. Much of it found its way into the jail cells at the back of the sheriff's office.

The train arrived from Helena three times a week. Like clockwork, so did the inappropriate behavior, the drunks, and the thieves. He sighed. The moment the train stopped and the doors opened, evil would step foot on the platform.

Wyatt could feel it in the air. Evil was here. He glanced about. All he saw was local women hurrying off the train and into the arms of their husbands. Their arms were laden with packages. Many packages.

He vowed never to marry. It was too dangerous for the wives of lawmen, besides, marriage wasn't for him.

Still, those men looked pleased to see their wives, even if they had only been gone a day or two. Wyatt shook his head. He was steadfast in his vow not to marry.

He didn't need a wife, anyway.

Chapter Two

Not far outside Halliwell Junction

Bridget Spencer's heart pounded. With her abductor asleep, she'd finally been able to slip out of his room. Except now she had nowhere to go.

She'd known Hugo Jacobs for many years. He'd courted her in her twenties, but Bridget wasn't interested. Hugo was a ruffian. Uncouth at best. Violent at his worst. He tried to guilt her into marrying him when she came of age, but Bridget resisted.

She had always seen herself as plain, and most of the men who came to see her were more interested in her father's money than Bridget herself.

Particularly after Father died.

The townsfolk tried desperately to convince her to marry. Especially those with single sons. Bridget knew it was her eventual inheritance they were really interested in, not a plain-looking spinster who had long passed the age of suitability.

All hope of ever marrying had left her mind long ago. Caring for her ailing mother for many years, when did they expect her to find the time to seek a husband? Had it not been so upsetting, it would have been laughable. After mother had passed, Bridget inherited a small fortune. The conditions of the will stated she could not receive her inheritance until she married.

She found it especially outrageous, given she was on the verge of forty. A spinster of the worst kind. One who had no hope of ever marrying for love.

Filling her days undertaking charitable work, Bridget hadn't actively sought a husband. Instead, per her father's will, she received a monthly allowance from her inheritance. It was enough to live on, but little more. Her charitable work could continue as a result.

Everyone in her hometown of Helena knew Bridget had no intention of marrying. She was happy with her life the way it was.

She shook herself mentally. Bridget did not know how much longer Hugo Jacobs would sleep. Thankful he hadn't bound her, and she crept out of the carriage he'd held her in.

Closing the door quietly, she hurried down the corridor looking for a way off the train. She opened the door where the carriages were joined and glanced about. She stepped outside onto the narrow platform between the carriages and glanced down at the coupling. The fast-moving train posed a threat to Bridget's life if she were to slip. Except Bridget knew her only chance of escape was to jump.

She had two choices – go back to the carriage and agree to marry Hugo, or jump and hope she could get her life back again.

Bridget took a deep breath. She glanced about again. If she jumped now, in the overgrown grass, the landing would be reasonably soft. She hoped.

It was now or never.

Bridget rolled into a ball as she jumped. Her heart was pounding so hard, she was certain it would jump right out of her chest. Never before had she as much as contemplated such a feat. She hoped she never had to again.

As she hit the ground, despite the length of the grass, her landing was not as soft as Bridget had hoped. Once she stopped rolling on the sloping hillside, she remained still for a minute or two, checking to ensure nothing was broken.

She'd had the foresight to snatch up her reticule before leaving the train, but had to forfeit the rest of her belongings, or risk Hugo catching her in the process of leaving. Except now, her reticule was nowhere to be seen.

Lifting her head slightly from the ground to ensure no one had seen her, Bridget was shocked to discover a man staring in her direction. She flattened herself against the ground, and stayed there, ensuring he didn't spot her.

Part of Hugo's strategy was to keep her awake. His plan, as far as she could tell, was to torture her with lack of sleep, erroneously believing she would eventually give into his demands. Bridget was nobody's fool, and saw right through him.

Bridget closed her eyes, and was soon fast asleep. When she awoke, she was shocked to discover the sun was setting. Luckily there was still enough daylight for her to search for her reticule. It had to be here somewhere, and Bridget was determined to find it.

On her hands and knees, despite the smattering of snow, she scoured the area, hoping to find her reticule in a nearby copse of trees. Despite the pain in her ankle, Bridget crawled around the area, trying to locate her belongings.

This was not the way Bridget intended to use her hard-earned freedom, but it was out of her control. Moments later, the setting sun glinted off something shiny. Could it be her reticule? It was important she find it. How would she survive otherwise? Crawling low to ensure she wasn't seen, Bridget finally located the missing reticule.

In the process of landing where it had, her reticule opened, and her meagre belongings were spread about, and were nowhere to be seen. It was enough to make her cry. Except Bridget was celebrating getting away from Hugo Jacobs, so she refused to let even one tear fall.

"Everything has to be here," she muttered as she scouted around trying to locate her missing belongings. The most important items, at least in Bridget's mind, were her bank book and money. Not that she'd had a lot of cash with her, but it would get her a warm bed for a short time, and see her fed. Perhaps she might even have a little left over. No matter what, she needed to be frugal with what little money she had. If she found her belongings, that was.

A small portion of her money was inside, but the remainder was nowhere to be seen. Her bank book was also missing, as was her hair brush, and a small photograph of her parents, both now deceased.

Most of her remaining possessions were lightweight, which meant they could have spread over a large area. She wasn't giving up until she found everything. She was left with so little, Bridget was determined to retrieve it all.

She continued to crawl around, despite the knowledge her gown would be filthy by the time she finished. One thing Bridget was certain – she could not stay out here overnight. It was already chilly, and thin layers of snow were scattered about.

And yet, despite everything, she felt safe. When Hugo awoke, he would know she was gone, but thankfully, would have no idea where she left the train.

The truth was, Bridget also did not know where she was.

Chapter Three

With the reassurance no one untoward had arrived today, Wyatt headed back to the sheriff's office. He was still perplexed about what he thought he'd seen earlier in the day. He couldn't have imagined a woman falling from the train. *Could he?* Wyatt shook his head, trying to shake the feeling there was more to it.

Although he had to admit, he was quite a distance from the railway line. Still, his eyesight was good. Unlike some people his age, he didn't need spectacles. When he turned forty, the traveling eye doctor insisted he would need spectacles, but Wyatt had proven him wrong. In his line of work, spectacles would be nothing but a nuisance.

Making himself a coffee, he still pondered over the woman he believed he saw jump from the train. His mind was *not* playing tricks on him, Wyatt was absolutely certain of it. Despite the chill in the air, Wyatt pulled on his thick jacket and took his coffee outside. That way he could keep an eye out and ensure peace prevailed.

He glanced at the thin layer of snow, and knew it would get worse soon. This close to Christmas, it was usually thicker. One thing Wyatt knew, they would definitely have a white Christmas. They always did.

Bringing the mug to his lips, Wyatt took a mouthful of coffee. He enjoyed sitting out here at sunset - it was his favorite time of day. Even despite the cold.

Out of the corner of his eye, something caught his attention. What it was, he couldn't be certain. He slammed the mug onto the side table, and stood.

Today was turning out to be the exact opposite of what he preferred. A day of peace and quiet.

Wishing he hadn't seen anything on the hillside, not now and not earlier, Wyatt trudged up the mostly unused area. He'd had a few criminal types jump off the train before it reached the platform, but never had he seen a woman do so.

It made him question his sanity. What kind of woman would jump from a moving train? There were only two scenarios, a criminal, which was rare for women, but did happen. The other type was a desperate female trying to escape something or someone.

Ensuring himself his Colt was in its holster where it belonged, Wyatt near ran up the hill. At least that was the plan. He got about halfway and realized if he didn't slow down, he would be out of breath and not able to round anyone up. Especially not someone who was on the run.

He scoured the area where he thought he'd seen her jump, but found nothing. As he moved closer, Wyatt was convinced he was right. A patch of overgrown grass was flattened to the shape of a person. She must have lain there for some time, since the grass had still not sprung back into place.

Except now there was no sign of her.

Wyatt shrugged his shoulders and began to walk away. As much as he wanted to find the woman today, darkness would descend soon. He'd only gone a few steps when he heard an unfamiliar sound. What it was, he had no idea. It wasn't a bird or even a critter he was certain.

Was the woman hiding from him? The trees and bushes would give her plenty of coverage. This time of night, Wyatt didn't relish searching the area. On the other hand, without enough clothing and blankets a person could, and probably would, perish in this weather.

His conscience got the better of him, and Wyatt continued his search. Trouble was, the trees were overgrown on the hillside. No one ever cut it back, because, well, it was an area no one ever used. Luckily for the woman, where she'd leaped from the train was mostly clear of overgrowth. Either side of the grassy knoll lay bushes and low hanging trees. Had she landed there, she could have been seriously injured.

It made Wyatt even more determined to do a thorough search before the light completely disappeared. He didn't fancy going back down the hillside in the dark. There was no pathway back into town, and no rail for anyone to take hold of. Why would there be? It wasn't an area where anyone was expected to wander about, let alone jump from a moving train.

It had been pure luck on Wyatt's part he'd even witnessed the woman jump. Another few minutes and he would have missed it altogether.

Chapter Four

Bridget froze.

Someone was nearby. Her heart pounded at the thought of Hugo Jacobs finding her. She slapped a hand to her mouth to stop herself from screaming. Or even making a sound. Her breathing was heavy, and she wondered if it would give her position away.

As much as the cold was settling in for the night, Bridget couldn't risk being found. Hugo was determined to force her into marriage for no other reason but to steal her inheritance. She didn't care about the money. It was never important to her. If it was, she could have married years ago.

She was waiting to find the right person. After all, once her inheritance came through, it became the property of her husband. Bridget had no intention of providing Hugo with her father's hard-earned money. He was a criminal through and through. He would never change, and they both knew it.

Staying as quiet as she could, Bridget heard movement again. She silently prayed it wasn't

Hugo, except she was certain it was. Her biggest regret was not stealing his gun, but she didn't want to risk him waking up. If he had awoken, she wouldn't be here now.

It might not be the safest place to hide, but there was so much overgrowth, and she was well hidden under the bushes.

Her heart pounding even louder than she thought possible, Bridget slapped her other hand over her mouth.

She was quivering, but Bridget wasn't sure if it was from fear or the cold. It could even be both.

Then she realized – the movement had stopped. Should she risk peeking out between the foliage to check. She was torn. Her mind was moving all over the place, and with her heart pounding so fast, she was now feeling lightheaded. Not being able to breathe through her mouth probably wasn't helping.

After what seemed an eternity, Bridget was certain Hugo had gone. He was an impatient man, and always gave up easily. Except this time, he'd harassed Bridget until he found an opportunity to snatch her when no one else saw. He had a gun on her until the moment they boarded the train. After that, Hugo believed she had no means of escape. Besides, he'd warned her, no one would believe she'd been kidnapped.

Suddenly there was movement again. "I can see you in there," an unfamiliar voice said. "Come out now or I will shoot."

Bridget gasped. She was well hidden. How was she found? Except it wasn't Hugo. Had he sent one of his cronies to find her?

There was no other option than to leave her hiding place. Not that she'd been very well hidden. She'd been found and that was not conducive to her wellbeing. Bridget tried to stand, her heart throbbing. The first time Hugo took her, she hadn't felt this bad. She decided it was worse because she'd managed to get away.

There would be no second chances, she was certain. Hugo would have her bound hands and feet this time. And likely gag her as well. He wouldn't risk having her get away a second time.

"I won't say it again," the stranger said. "Show yourself." The click of his gun being readied told Bridget he was serious. Her head was pounding, and her heart racing. She wasn't even sure she could stand up.

"I…alright," she said, her voice wavering. Except when she finally tried to stand she couldn't. Bridget was weak from lack of food, and more likely than not, she was covered in bruises. For a while, she contemplated letting him kill her. That was preferable to marrying Hugo who was a tyrant. "Just shoot me," she finally said, her voice breaking as she spoke. "That is my preference. I am not prepared to marry Hugo Jacobs. He's nothing but a bully. He will take my inheritance then find a way to kill me anyway." She sighed, and hoped her death would be over and done with quickly.

Bridget stopped moving and waited for the bullet to hit. She only hoped he did the job properly the first time.

"Lady," the stranger said. "I don't know what you're talking about. "Allow me introduce myself. Wyatt Hawkins. *Sheriff* Wyatt Hawkins," he said. "I'm here to help you."

Tears sprang to Bridget's eyes. Was it true? Was this man going to save her? Rescue her from certain death with Hugo? When the tears came, so did the sobs. She crawled out from her hiding place, hoping the stranger was telling the truth.

Bridget still couldn't believe Hugo hadn't sent someone to kill her, although he was certainly capable of it. The man who stood before her, now squatted down to her level. He wore a sheriff's badge, so she had to believe he was genuine.

Still sobbing, he handed her a handkerchief, and put a hand to her back. Those were not the actions of a murderer. It instilled trust, and was the last thing

Bridget expected. After all she'd been through, trust was not one of her traits.

"What happened here?" he asked gently, his hand still on her back. He'd long put away the gun the moment he realized she wasn't a threat. "Tell me why you jumped from the train this morning."

"I…what I said before," she said, her sobs now settling. "I was kidnapped for my inheritance. Hugo Jacobs. A man I know well."

"He forced you to marry him?" The sheriff's words were quiet, but held disbelief.

"That was the plan. He wanted to wait until we arrived at a town where no one knew either of us." Saying it all out loud had her heart thumping again. "I would like to get out of here in case he returns, looking for me."

"If you were kidnapped, how did you get away?" He still sounded skeptical, and Bridget couldn't help but believe no assistance would be forthcoming in this town. He waved a hand in front of himself. "This can wait. Let's get you down the hillside. I'll have the doc check you over, then we can talk."

"My belongings. They are few, but I…I need to find them." Bridget glanced about. It was almost dark now and the only light available was from the moon.

"Let me worry about that. I'd rather you got medical attention first. I'll find your belongings, I promise."

Perhaps the sheriff wasn't so bad after all.

Chapter Five

Wyatt couldn't believe what was happening. This woman, this stranger, who had jumped from a moving train to escape, was still in one piece. At least she seemed that way on the surface.

"Let me help you to your feet," Wyatt said, holding both her hands, and assisting her to stand up. "Have you broken any bones?" he asked, genuinely concerned.

She glanced up at him. Even in the darkness, he could see the concern on her face. Not that he blamed her. "I…I don't think so," she said, but seemed quite weak. Would she be able to make it down the hillside?

It wasn't as steep as some, but certainly wasn't flat. If she couldn't get there under her own steam, Wyatt wasn't sure how he would get her down and into town. "I will help you," he said gently, then reached out to her, taking one hand, and putting an arm around her.

He wasn't a doctor, but it was clear to Wyatt she had been injured in the process of escaping. He had never jumped from a moving train, and never wanted to either. He glanced across, and saw the concern on her face. Surely she was pleased to be getting out of the bushes? If he could find her there, anyone could.

"Not long to go now," he said, trying to encourage the stranger to continue. She winced, and it confirmed his suspicions – she was in pain. Wyatt wasn't surprised. It was quite a feat she'd undertaken. If what she said was true, he expected there could be sprains or even broken bones, not to mention other injuries.

She breathed a sigh of relief when they came to flat ground. Wyatt did too. Doc's office wasn't far now, but he had no intention of letting her continue to walk. It must have been pure torture for her coming down that hill.

He could have formed a posse to get her down the hill, but if what she said was true, the fewer people who knew she was in town, the better. Wyatt leaned in and picked her up. "Oh," he said. "I didn't ask your name." He gazed at her then, but she said nothing.

"It's safer for you and this town if I don't say," she said firmly, then turned away from him.

"You know I'll find out one way or another. You might as well tell me." Wyatt could be determined too.

She stared up at him, and he felt as though she would never stop checking him over. "Bridget," she whispered. "Bridget Spencer." A tear rolled down her face as though he had just signed her death warrant.

~*~

"What's the damage, Doc?" Wyatt asked, after Doctor Walker returned to the waiting area.

"Her left ankle is sprained, but should be fine in a few days. She is covered in bruises, and appears to be malnourished." The doc paused then, and ran a hand through his reclining hair. "More than that, she's been through a lot. The man who held her captive, deprived her of sleep." Doc Walker shook his head. "According to Miss Spencer, her kidnapper used it as a form of torture. Hoping she would give into his demands."

Wyatt's heart rate increased, and his anger rose. He had seen a lot of awful things over the years as a sheriff, but nothing like this. How did someone do that to another person? It never ceased to surprise him the things criminals would do for money.

"What happens now?" Wyatt asked, trying to keep a cool head when what he really wanted was to find this Hugo Jacobs and throw him in jail.

"I'm keeping Miss Spencer overnight to ensure nothing untoward happens."

Wyatt didn't hesitate. "I'll be here too. I need to stand guard in case her kidnapper returns. He sounds more than a little determined."

"I won't argue with that," Doc Walker told him.

"I promised Miss Spencer I would find her belongings. They were scattered when she jumped from the train. It's too dark now, so it will have to wait until morning."

Doc Walker nodded. "Of course. No one would expect you to go out tonight. Apart from it being an impossible task, who's to stay the kidnapper is not around?"

"Thanks, Doc," Wyatt said, and slapped the doc on the shoulder before taking a seat in the waiting room. He would stay until morning when his deputy would take over.

It had been a long night, and Wyatt was certain he'd drifted off to sleep more than once. He was annoyed with himself, and had gone into the room where Miss Spencer was sleeping. He stood in the doorway, listening to her breathing. He needed assurance she was still alive.

What if this Hugo Jacobs had discovered where she was and came back for her? It was something Wyatt couldn't allow. Not under any circumstances.

After glancing about the room, and checking under the bed, Wyatt went back to his seat in the waiting area. It was not right for him to be in a woman's room while she slept. Although under the circumstances, surely no one would accuse him of compromising the stranger?

Wyatt was restless. He could see the sun rising through one of the front windows. He stood again and glanced outside. It was quiet as he expected. No one else was out and about at this early time, not even the doc.

As Wyatt turned away, he saw something out the corner of his eye. He quickly turned back. There was nothing there. Perhaps it was a bird simply going about its business. Nonetheless, Wyatt stood watching for some time afterwards. The street was bare, and he put it down to tiredness.

It simply wouldn't do, and Wyatt knew it. He would get one of his deputies to take over sooner rather than later. Before he could have any sleep, Wyatt needed to retrieve Miss Spencer's belongings from the area where she'd jumped.

He still couldn't believe she'd done that. Even the strongest man would have thought twice before contemplating such an action. Except in this case, she knew it was her last chance. Wyatt couldn't blame Bridget Spencer one little bit.

Chapter Six

Bridget was certain someone had entered her room during the night. She was afraid of Hugo returning, and kidnapping her once again. Her biggest fear was not having him take her inheritance, it was what he would do to her afterwards.

Hugo Jacobs was not the kindest of men.

It was already clear to Bridget he would force her into marriage, take her money, then find a way to kill her. Of course, it wouldn't look like murder. Hugo would come up with a plan that would leave him appearing to be the innocent party in her death.

She may *fall* from a buggy, or *slip* over a cliff while they were out sightseeing on their *honeymoon*. The very thought of it had her heart racing. No matter what else she did, Bridget had to keep a low profile. Before she jumped, Bridget had no idea how small Halliwell Junction was. She would have been better off had she landed in a large city, where she could hide in plain sight.

Here? It was the complete opposite. Even the main street was small. There were ten stores at most.

The Lawman's Unwelcome Christmas Bride

From the little she'd seen last night, the town seemed isolated. She didn't know if there were any other towns close by.

Was there a stagecoach service? Perhaps she could buy a ticket and keep moving? Except that relied on the sheriff finding her belongings. Especially her money, little as it was.

The sheriff seemed a reasonable man. Perhaps he could advise her on where to go. He may know a town where she wouldn't stand out. She would listen to him. One thing Bridget did know, and that was she couldn't return home. Not that Hugo would expect her to go there, but he would eventually give up, and find her there.

Her life was no longer her own. Bridget had to come up with a plan to keep safe. When she was up to it, she would talk with the sheriff.

Merely thinking about Hugo and his plans for her exhausted Bridget. She closed her eyes and immediately fell asleep again.

When she opened her eyes again, Doc Walker was standing next to the bed. "Good morning," he said gently. "How are you feeling today?" He placed a stethoscope on her chest and listened, then looked into her eyes, then pulling down her bottom eyelid. Lastly, the doc checked her pulse. "You look far better this morning, and everything seems to be in order. I need to check your bandage and ensure it's firm enough."

He turned and began to walk away, but Bridget called him back. "Doctor Walker, is the sheriff still here?"

"I'm afraid not," the doc said. "He left a short time ago. Sheriff Hawkins had gone to find your belongings."

"Thank you," she said quietly, grateful the sheriff had done as he promised. "I hope it's not too cold outside. I'd hate for him to get a chill because of me."

Doc Walker chuckled. "We're used to this weather around this area. Wyatt will have rugged up before he left. I'll arrange for some breakfast for you, then I'll check your ankle." This time he hurried out of the room, and left Bridget alone.

The room was quiet, and Bridget could hear every minute sound from within the building. It put her on alert. What if Hugo worked out where she had jumped off the train, and was on his way to kidnapper her again? Bridget couldn't bear if she was taken captive again. With a sprained ankle, he would have more control over her than he did before.

Panic took over, and Bridget sat up in the bed, trying to slow her breathing. Moments later an older woman entered the room. She studied Bridget before placing the breakfast tray on a side table. "What's wrong, dear?" she asked, but Bridget was unable to answer. "I am the doctor's wife, Hilda Walker." She placed a hand on Bridget's shoulder. "I know your situation is difficult, but let's try and slow your breathing down." She moved her hand to Bridget's back. "I want you to breath in through your nose, and out through your mouth. Slowly, like this." Hilda demonstrated, and Bridget copied her. Soon her breathing was back to normal.

"Thank you for helping me," Bridget said quietly. She was embarrassed about her lack of control. The thought of Hugo finding her and snatching her all over again was enough to panic anyone. Even the most calm person. It made her wonder if the sheriff was on edge, too.

She shook away the thought almost the moment it came to her mind. Sheriff Hawkins would not be worried about a small time criminal like Hugo. Except she had to acknowledge, Hugo was now in the big time. Kidnapping was not a misdemeanor by any means. If caught, he could spend the rest of his life in jail. He could even be hanged.

A shiver when through her.

"Are you alright, dear?" Mrs. Walker asked. Bridget nodded, and the doctor's wife passed over her breakfast. "Take your time. There is no hurry."

She wasn't so hungry as Bridget thought she would be, but the mug of tea really appealed to her.

Moments later, the older woman was gone.

It felt strange to have her ankle bandaged. Doc Walker handed over some crutches. He showed Bridget how to use them, and told her she needed to be careful not to fall while using them.

It was nice to know people at Halliwell Junction cared about her wellbeing. She was still a bit wobbly on the crutches, but according to Mrs. Walker, it wouldn't take long for her to get used to them.

The door behind her suddenly opened, and she spun around, forgetting the crutches. Both Mrs. Walker and the doctor steadied her.

"I apologize," Sheriff Hawkins said. "I didn't mean to startle you." He moved closer, and Bridget noticed her reticule in his hands. "I'm not sure how much money you had, but this was all I could find. I found your other belongings, too," he said, stopping when the doctor held up a hand for him to keep a distance from the injured woman.

"We are practicing walking on crutches," Doc Walker informed him. "If you can wait, we're almost done."

The sheriff nodded his acceptance, then sat down out of the way. Bridget glanced across at him. He didn't seem happy. Was that because he'd spent part of his morning looking for her meagre belongings? She'd told him the previous night it was all she managed to salvage from the train.

Now though, Bridget wasn't sure what she would do. She saw nothing last night that even slightly resembled a boarding house. Was that why the sheriff appeared so unhappy? Because he didn't know what he would do with her?

This entire situation was turning into a disaster. Bridget could see the writing on the wall – he would ship her off to another town. Another destination, where she would be their problem, and no longer his concern.

Chapter Seven

With every passing minute, Wyatt worried. It was clear Bridget needed protection. She also needed somewhere to stay.

The one and only option was the saloon, and there was no way he could allow her to stay there. It simply wasn't safe. The proof was in the jail cells. Last night there was a fight at the saloon. His deputy arrested the two drunks involved. They would be released sometime this morning.

He was right in not wanting her to stay in *that* place. Besides, she wouldn't be able to navigate the stairs to the accommodation. Not to mention the shenanigans that went on there. Most of the rooms were hired by the hour, not the day. A real lady should not be privy to the depravity of the saloon.

His mind made up, Wyatt stood. It seemed the lesson on crutches was over, and he needed to get a statement from Miss Spencer. "I hate to be a bother," he said, ensuring she heard. "I do need to get a statement from you. Would you accompany me to the sheriff's office?"

She appeared bewildered. "I…how am I supposed to get there?" she asked quietly. "I am barely managing to stay upright on the floor. The *flat* floor," she said, emphasizing flat.

She had a point, and the solution baffled Wyatt, but only for a short time. Stepping toward the injured woman, Wyatt slipped an arm beneath her, and picked Miss Spencer up. "I'll carry you there." It was the perfect solution.

When he glanced down into her face, Wyatt noticed her scowl. Why was she not happy with his solution? It was perfect for the situation.

"Put me down," she quietly ground out, but he decided to ignore her pleas.

How else did she expect to get to the sheriff's office? It was slippery from the snow, and she would never make it on crutches without falling. Heck, he nearly went head first on his way here. "No Ma'am," he said firmly. "It's too dangerous for you on crutches."

Mrs. Walker held the front door open and handed the patient her crutches. Wyatt carried the determined Miss Bridget Spencer onto the boardwalk. It was snowing. Not as heavily as it would get, but heavy enough to make the road even more slippery than it was before.

Wyatt sighed.

This was going to be more difficult than he expected, but he'd take it slowly. That way they would both get there in one piece.

What would normally be a short stroll across the road turned out to be a far longer trip. Wyatt had to avoid areas that appeared icy, and therefore dangerous. The last thing he wanted was to harm the woman further. She was in a bad enough condition as it was.

Finally they reached their destination, and he opened the door to his office, and placed her on a chair. By this point, Wyatt could see she was fuming, but she hadn't said a word. She'd been through so much recently, according to what she'd told him last night, and he thought she would be more vocal about her feelings.

Perhaps she was simply too exhausted to complain. It was probably what Hugo Jacobs had counted on. As much as it was awful she'd had to jump from that train to save her life, perhaps Miss Spencer had realized she was on the verge of breaking.

He ensured she was comfortable, then went around to the other side of the desk. Wyatt reached for his interview pad, then found a pencil in the top drawer. "I apologize, Miss Spencer, but I do need you to start over again. Your statement needs to be complete." He glanced down at the pad, pencil poised, and waited for her to begin. Except she didn't. "Is everything alright, Miss Spencer?" he asked gently.

Wyatt wasn't one of those sheriffs who bullied people into giving information. It wasn't in him to do that. He reached across the desk, and patted her hand. "It will be alright. We'll find this Hugo Jacobs and incarcerate him."

She frowned. "You don't know that," she bit out. "He's done some terrible things in his life, and is yet to be punished."

Under his hand, he could feel her quivering. Whether that was from being afraid, or from anger, Wyatt didn't know. "This time will be different," he said. "I don't tolerate this sort of behavior in my town." He sat back and crossed his arms. No longer touching her, it felt as a part of him was missing.

Wyatt had no intention of going there. He had been unattached for most of his life. He'd had a girlfriend here and there, but they hadn't sparked any feelings in him. Now that he had breached forty, Wyatt was no longer interested in women. Who would want an aging sheriff anyway?

She studied him. "How do I know I can trust you?" Her words were quiet yet forceful. It was clear Miss Spencer had been let down many times before. Had this Hugo Jacobs harassed her prior to this incident? Her kidnapping?

Wyatt felt anger rise through him. Her terror, her indignation, became his. If it was the last thing he did, Wyatt would get justice for Bridget Spencer.

~*~

With the paperwork done, Wyatt could now get her settled, except where was she meant to stay? With no Inn or boarding house in town, it was impossible. Besides, she was going to need protection day and night. If her abductor was as bad as she'd said, he couldn't risk not having her covered twenty-four hours a day.

"I'll work something out for your accommodation," Wyatt said. As soon as the words were out, his deputy arrived. He would protect Miss Spencer while Wyatt got some sleep. "A word," he said to the deputy, then went into a side room where they could talk privately.

"Is everything alright, Sheriff?" Deputy Jonah Simpson asked. Wyatt had filled the man in on the situation earlier. But neither man had thought about her accommodation.

Wyatt shook his head. "I'm not sure what do to with her. There is nowhere in town for Miss Spencer to stay." He scratched his head as he tried to think.

"It's a dilemma, for sure," the deputy said. "What about your place?" He raised his eyebrows and Wyatt knew it was the perfect solution.

Except for one thing – it would ruin Miss Spencer's reputation. And he couldn't have that.

Chapter Eight

Bridget couldn't help it. As much as she didn't want to leave Halliwell Junction, if they had nowhere for her to stay, she had to go.

She watched as the sheriff and his deputy left her alone to talk. They spoke in whispers, and she couldn't make out the words. Despite being in the next room. It felt as though there was a conspiratory, and she was in the middle of it.

Worse still, they were talking about her. Now she was fuming. She pulled herself to a standing position and reached for her crutches.

She could do this. Or at least give it her best shot.

Hobbling over to the doorway, it appeared neither man had noticed her. It was Bridget's intent – she hoped to catch them out, arranging her life without giving her a choice. Well, they could forget it! Bridget made her own decisions, and didn't need men to tell her what to do.

"…sheriff's accommodations," the deputy said, but Bridget hadn't heard the beginning of the sentence. What had she missed?

Sheriff Hawkins didn't look happy, and scowled. "She won't go for your idea, and frankly, I'm not sure I do either."

Bridget cleared her throat, causing both men's heads to spin around in her direction. "I don't get a say in any of this?" she said firmly, letting her displeasure known. Bridget decided to leave the room and let them arrange whatever. She was not interested, no matter what they organized. It wasn't up to the two lawmen to dictate her life. "You're no better than Hugo," she said, then spun around, forgetting she was on crutches.

As she fell to the ground, Sheriff Hawkins moved far more quickly than Bridget thought possible. His arms were quickly around her, stopping Bridget from falling. The crutches fell to the ground as he lifted her, and carried Bridget back to the chair she'd sat on only moments before.

He pulled up a chair and sat facing her, only inches away. "We have a dilemma," he said gently. "There is nowhere here for you to stay. The saloon isn't safe, not by any means." He ran a hand through his hair, then studied her. "My deputy says I should take you to the sheriff's cottage. It's right next door."

"No," she said firmly.

The sheriff sighed. "I can protect you there, day and night."

"It is not happening," she said forcefully. "I would like to maintain whatever reputation I still have left."

Sheriff Hawkins shrugged his shoulders. "There's nowhere else in town for you to go." He sounded worried for her.

Bridget was also worried about her situation. "Is there another town nearby? One that has a women's boarding house?" That would work, but it wouldn't alter the fact she was in danger from Hugo finding her. She still needed protection. It always came back to the same thing.

The sheriff reached out and held her hand. "I could relocate you. Of course I could. But I couldn't stay and provide the protection you require." Still holding her hand, he closed his eyes. Was he thinking about an alternative plan?

It had become clear to Bridget she couldn't leave town. She also couldn't stay with the sheriff. If he were married and she was a guest, it would be different. There would be no compromising her. But with both of them unattached, it was a completely different scenario.

Then a thought struck her. He could be married – she had no idea either way. "Are you married," she asked, staring at him. She had made assumptions that may not be true. He was a good looking man, and was more than likely married. He suddenly pulled his hand away from hers, and sat straighter. He'd leaned in while he tried to coerce her into staying with him.

"I'm not," he said firmly, then closed his eyes again. Moments later, he opened them. This time they were wide with anticipation. "We can fix this," he said quietly. Bridget couldn't see how. She'd already been told there was no accommodation available for her in town. "Miss Spencer, will you marry me?" Bridget stared at the man who was unexpectedly proposing. "Miss Spencer, Bridget?" he asked again, only this time more forcefully. "Having a different surname will keep you safe."

Bridget became lightheaded with shock. The sheriff was right. It would keep her safe, but did she really want to marry him for it to happen?

~*~

Waiting for the preacher to arrive, Bridget still couldn't believe she'd agreed to marry Sheriff Hawkins. Er, Wyatt. As a married couple, they couldn't address each other so formally, he explained before the deputy fetched the preacher. He was also tasked with getting Mrs. Walker to the sheriff's office as a witness.

Agreeing to a marriage of convenience took the sting out of being practically forced to agree to this marriage. It would save her life, Wyatt reiterated, noting her reluctance. Besides, they could get their marriage annulled when the danger was over.

Bridget agreed based on those conditions.

The door to the sheriff's office opened. Mrs. Walker stared at Wyatt. "You don't expect your bride to marry in those grubby clothes do you?" she asked, although it sounded more like a demand. "I'll be back shortly with a new gown from the mercantile. My clothes would be far too small for her."

Bridget heard him sigh. "Put it on my account," he said moments before she closed the door.

Hilda Walker called over her shoulder. "I fully intended to," she said, laughter in her voice. Then she was gone.

The moment the older woman was back, she took Bridget to an adjoining room and fussed over her. Mrs. Walker ensured Bridget looked her best for her wedding. Not that she knew it was a marriage of convenience, but she probably guessed. At least Bridget assumed she'd worked it out. Mrs. Walker was not stupid.

Instead of the sheriff's office, Mrs. Walker insisted they use the side room. There were files in there, but nothing more, and seemed ideal.

Mrs. Walker opened the door. "You may come in now," she said when Bridget was cleaned up and in fresh clothes.

When Wyatt entered the room, his steps faltered. Was he having second thoughts already? Or did something else cause him to stumble? Bridget couldn't help but wonder. He'd not married until now, and she was certain he only did so now under duress. "You look beautiful," he whispered when he finally stood beside her. Warmth flooded Bridget. He reached for her hands, and held them gently to his chest, causing her heart to flutter.

If she didn't know better, Bridget would believe this man, this near stranger who was about to become her husband, was in love with her.

Chapter Nine

Wyatt clutched both of Bridget's hands. Not only did it give him comfort, but he was determined to protect her. This stranger he was about to marry.

Her blue eyes were mesmerizing, and he wanted to reach out and stroke her cheek. At the last minute, Wyatt refrained from making this personal. He mentally shook himself – he didn't want to marry. Not now and not ever. He'd been a sheriff for the majority of his adult life. From the day his sheriff's badge was pinned to his chest, he vowed not to marry.

It wasn't for his benefit, but for that of any potential wife. A sheriff's life was a dangerous one. Any given day could be his last. He could literally walk out of his office this very moment and get shot by a deranged criminal. The thought had him shuddering.

What had he let Bridget into, suggesting they marry? For all he knew, Hugo Jacobs could have already located his bride, and could be waiting outside for her. It was all the more reason she needed protection.

Or the man could be waiting for Wyatt. Then what good would he be to Bridget? A shiver shot down his spine.

"Are you alright?" Bridget whispered in his ear. Her warm breath had his insides quivering. Not in a bad way. He was frozen with fear for her, and couldn't answer. Bridget pulled one of her hands out of his grip, and caressed his cheek.

He stared into her beautiful face. As much as he liked what she was doing to him, Wyatt knew he had to keep his distance. It would be far too easy to fall in love with the woman he was about to marry for her own protection.

He leaned close to her face. "I'm…fine," he lied. How could he tell Bridget he was already having feelings for her? They'd only know each other a short time. Far too short a time for him to genuinely feel anything for her.

The preacher cleared his throat. "Are we ready?" he asked firmly, alerting Wyatt the man was losing patience. He wasn't normally that way, so perhaps he had other things to do back at the church.

"We are," Wyatt said. "Apologies for the delay, Preacher."

Instead of answering, the preacher went straight into the marriage ceremony. "Dearly beloved," he began. Ten minutes later, Wyatt and Bridget were husband and wife.

~*~

Wyatt unlocked the door to the sheriff's office, after checking having his deputy check it was safe for Bridget. She stood next to him, waiting to enter her new home. Even if it was temporary, in line with their marriage being short term, which suited Wyatt. He had no intention of being tied down to a wife.

Hence the reason he was still single at forty-two years of age.

He glanced down at his new wife and smiled. She really was beautiful. Except she was sad. Being forced into marriage was not the best way to start off. His heart fluttered, and Wyatt didn't know why.

It was clear from the moment they met he liked her. But like and love were two different things. It wasn't even twenty-four hours since they'd met. She was in a really bad way when he found her. She still was. Right now, she was clinging to her crutches, and waiting to go inside. He reached over and took her crutches, leaning them up against the wall.

His heart now pounding, Wyatt lifted her, and carried the petite woman across the threshold, such as it was. "What...? Why did you do that?" she whispered, her warm breath on his cheek increasing his heart rate even more.

"I…" Wyatt put her down once they were inside, then retrieved her crutches. "Every new bride should be carried across the threshold of her new home."

"Except this marriage is a farce. Neither of us want it." She was firm in her words, and it shattered Wyatt's heart. He couldn't fathom why.

"I know," he said quietly. "What if you never marry again? You will have missed out on the experience."

"There is a very good reason I have never married," she said, annoyance clear in her voice. "Most men have been after my inheritance and not interested in me."

Now Wyatt was getting annoyed. "Is that what you think? I want your money?" He ran a hand across his chin, his irritation growing. "I don't want your inheritance. My only motivation is to keep you safe without ruining your reputation." Despite himself, Wyatt picked her up again, and carried Bridget to the sitting room. There he placed her on the most comfortable chair and moved a low table close by to elevate her leg. It was what the doc instructed.

Except it looked uncomfortable. He left the room to get a pillow. "That's better," he said, placing it so

Bridget was more comfy. He wondered why he'd bothered when she was being unreasonable. "Would you like tea or coffee?" He was partway out of the room before she had a chance to answer.

"Tea would be nice," she called. Wyatt heard her sigh. Not only did he have to protect her, but he also had to put up with her unfounded accusations and bad temper. Not to mention he would need to cook for his new wife until her ankle healed.

Wasn't that what a husband was expected to do when his wife was incapacitated? He knew how to cook, but was no chef. It would be far better – for both of them – if she was able to cook instead.

~*~

The atmosphere in the sitting room was icy, and so was the temperature. Wyatt added logs to the fireplace, along with kindling and scrunched up newspaper. Bridget had been quiet, mostly because she slept. He had set up the spare bedroom for her, but didn't have the heart to wake her. After discovering she had been tortured with sleep deprivation, Wyatt knew she needed the rest.

Except she didn't look as comfortable as he would have liked. Against his better judgement, Wyatt crept over to where Bridget slept and gently picked her up. As he lifted her, she screamed. And screamed. And screamed some more. All the time her eyes remained tightly shut.

His first instinct was to slap a hand over her mouth, but that would only make things worse, Wyatt was certain. "Bridget," he whispered. "It's Wyatt."

She finally opened her eyes and stared up at him. Bridget's breath whooshed out in relief as she saw his face. A hand went to her chest. "I…I'm sorry. I thought Hugo had found me."

Her reaction cut through Wyatt's heart. "I decided to take you to bed. You looked so uncomfortable asleep on the chair."

She lifted a hand and caressed his cheek, but quickly pulled it back. "I'm sorry," she said quietly. "For everything."

She had nothing to be sorry for, but Wyatt nodded. If it made her happy to apologize, then so be it. "I made up the bed for you," he said, and continued toward the spare room. "I'll light the fire in there once you are settled. It can get quite chilly in the cottage this time of year."

"Thank you," Bridget said, and opened her mouth to speak again, but quickly closed it. It made Wyatt wonder what she'd intended to say.

Chapter Ten

Bridget glanced up at her new husband. She knew it wasn't necessary, but she needed to apologize. She had upended his life in one foul swoop. Or as it turned out, from her act of jumping from a train.

The fact she was married now meant she was no longer prey for Hugo. Except he didn't know that. She wanted to tell Wyatt, but was far too tired to go into a prolonged discussion. She'd convinced herself it's what would result.

Already drifting off to sleep in his arms, Bridget knew this wasn't the time. After she was fully rested and alert, then they would discuss her inheritance, and not before.

Wyatt had pulled the bedding back, ready for her to get in. Instead of standing her on the cold floor, he placed her in the bed, then pulled the bedding up over her. Although she'd only lay there for mere moments, Bridget was enjoying the luxurious mattress and bedding. After sleeping on the hard train beds for goodness knew how long, this bed felt magnificent.

After ensuring she was settled, and had everything she needed, Wyatt squatted down in front of the fire, and stayed there until it was burning properly. She couldn't thank him enough, but Bridget was exhausted. She could barely think, let alone talk. It didn't take long and her eyes closed.

Soon she was in a slumberous sleep. Something she had needed for many days.

When she finally awoke, Bridget was confused about where she was. She lay on the luxurious bed, with her head on a feather-like pillow, and glanced about. It was warm and comfortable, which seemed to trigger a memory for her. Apart from the burning fire, the room was dark.

And yet Bridget was convinced she was safe. She had no idea why, but she did.

Footsteps headed her way, getting closer with each step. She lay quietly, not making a sound. Soon someone entered the room holding a lantern. "Oh good. You're awake. Did you sleep well? I checked a few times and you were in a deep sleep."

Bridget stared. It was difficult to make out his face, but the voice was familiar. "Who are you?" she asked, her voice thick with emotion.

She heard the man's intake of breath. One thing she did know, it wasn't Hugo. He was never that kind or polite. Not to her, nor anyone else. "Bridget," he said, as though confirming he knew who she was. "It's Wyatt. Sheriff Hawkins." He paused as though choosing his next words carefully. "I am your husband."

She gasped, then thought for a moment. "We married in the sheriff's office. I remember now."

He let out some more breath. Bridget understood how her not remembering could cause serious ramifications for him. "I've made supper, if you feel up to it." He placed the lantern on a side table then sat on the side of the bed. "It's not much. I put a stew together earlier today. I'm not a great cook."

Bridget reached out and took his hand. "Thank you. I appreciate all you've done for me. I just hope it doesn't get you killed."

Wyatt stared down into her face. "I contacted the marshals. They are looking for Hugo. The man needs to be punished for his actions. Unfortunately, we don't know how long it will take to locate him."

Was that regret because she was still in danger, or because he had been lumbered with looking out for her? No matter what, they'd agreed to an annulment at the end of it all. They hadn't discussed her inheritance at all, which now belonged to Wyatt. From the interaction she'd had with other men, she could safely assume that was the last she would see of her money.

"Are you alright?" Wyatt asked when she didn't say anything. His hand went to her forehead. "It doesn't feel like you have a fever. Are you in pain? Should I get the doc?"

"I don't need a doctor," she said firmly. "My concern lays with the marshals trying to find Hugo. He was willing to kill me for my inheritance. I am certain he would not flinch if confronted by marshals." Bridget sat upright in the bed. She felt hollow. Saving herself had caused others to be put in danger. It was the last thing she wanted.

"They can look after themselves. It's what they do." Wyatt stood then, and passed over her crutches. "Do you need help?" he asked, but she waved him aside.

As she reached the passageway, the aroma from the kitchen was enticing. Bridget hobbled her way toward the wonderful smell, ready to eat. She only hoped Wyatt was a decent enough cook.

"Oh, you even made biscuits!" Bridget said as she settled herself at the table. Wyatt took her crutches, then placed a plate of beef stew in front of her. Bridget stared down at the tempting food. "I can't eat this much," she protested. Wyatt frowned.

"Doc said you are malnourished and need to eat properly. Does that mean Hugo Jacobs starved you?" He sounded angry now, and Bridget didn't know why. He didn't know her. Not really. They might be married, but it was only for show. To stop Hugo forcing her into marriage. Wyatt had made that blatantly clear.

She didn't answer, and Wyatt didn't push her to respond, so Bridget took a mouthful of food instead. "This is good," she said. "Where did you learn to cook?"

"My mother was an excellent cook," Wyatt told her. "She gave me lessons when I decided to become a sheriff. Mother was aware of my plan to not marry."

His words had her stiffening her back. She was the reason he broke his solemn vow not to marry. And yet, here they were. "I'm sorry," she said quietly. "Perhaps we should arrange an annulment now, and once my sprained ankle is fine again, I'll disappear."

"It's not going to happen," he said, then tucked into his food. It was becoming clear that Wyatt Hawkins was not a man to be coerced. Not by her or anyone else.

Bridget wasn't sure if it was a good thing. She could be stubborn too.

Chapter Eleven

Wyatt ate slowly, taking the time to watch Bridget. Albeit covertly.

She pushed her food around the plate, but not much went in her mouth. Doc Walker explained it was important for her to eat well, since she was so malnourished.

Was it part of Hugo Jacobs plan to *eliminate* her once they married? Was it also part of his plan to have it appear she died from natural causes? Or even illness?

The mere thought of what the man had planned for Bridget made him shiver. His heart pounded, but Wyatt didn't know why. "There's plenty more where that came from," he said, but knew Bridget wouldn't eat more. She'd barely touched the food she already had.

"This is more than enough," she said quietly. Even if she ate only a quarter of what he'd dished up, Bridget would be doing well. Doc said it might take a while, and not to push her too much. Goodness knew how long she'd been kept prisoner, which meant it could have been weeks since she was kidnapped. He doubted even Bridget knew. "It is tasty," she said, then smiled briefly before taking another mouthful.

It was heartbreaking to watch. She was skin and bone. Wyatt felt certain she wasn't always like that. He would do everything in his power to not only keep her safe, but to fatten her up. Getting Bridget back to optimal health was important.

Wyatt wasn't sure why, but he believed his new bride was a strong woman. One who didn't allow anyone to push her around. It seemed her spirit had been broken, and it simply wouldn't do. Right now she went along with almost everything he said. He would rather have the real Bridget than a paper doll version of her.

What was she really like, he wondered? From the little he knew about her, Bridget had nursed her mother in her dying days. She'd refused several proposals of marriage, deciding to marry only for love. Hugo Jacobs had relentlessly pursued her within days of her mother's death. When his proposals hadn't worked, she'd been snatched by the known criminal.

Hugo apparently believed she was an easier target while Bridget was in mourning for her mother. He had been right. What sort of person did his vile behavior make him? In Wyatt's eyes he was a leach. Someone who sucked the life out of another.

Wyatt needed to know more about the kidnapper. He wondered if Hugo had family members helping him. As far as he was aware, the abductor didn't have a gang, and usually worked alone.

His thoughts were interrupted when a thin arm reached across the table for a biscuit. She couldn't quite reach, and he pushed the plate toward her. Their fingers touched as it reached her. He felt a zap, and quickly pulled his hand back. Bridget glanced up and stared at him, not saying a word. Wyatt didn't either, but he knew what it meant – he was attracted to the woman sitting opposite.

Only he knew it couldn't be true. They'd only met yesterday. He felt sorry for her, it was a fact. But there was no attraction between them. It wasn't even one-sided. She tolerated Wyatt simply because he was protecting her.

There was nothing more to it. Because he'd liked holding her in his arms counted for nothing. Her beautiful blue eyes enticing him meant little if anything at all. Her rosy lips and red hair counted for little.

No, Wyatt was not attracted to his pretend wife, and it would stay that way.

~*~

Bridget dozed in the sitting room while Wyatt cleaned up. She'd managed to eat little more than a mug full of the stew, but she ate two biscuits, which pleased him greatly. Hilda Walker had brought an apple pie for them, but Bridget refused it. He didn't push her. Perhaps tomorrow she might feel up to it.

At least tonight he knew she had something in her belly.

Since he was protecting Bridget, he would not be doing his regular sheriff duties. His two deputies would take over for the time being. Both he and Bridget would likely feel cooped up after a while, but until he knew Hugo Jacobs was safely behind bars, he wouldn't risk her going outside.

Once the kitchen was clean and tidy again, he joined his wife in the sitting room. She was still asleep. The criminal who snatched her had a lot to answer for. Doc didn't know specifics but said it could be days before she was back to her normal self. Perhaps even weeks.

Sleep deprivation was no joke. It had been used as a way of torture in the war, along with other forms of torture, such as starvation.

Hugo Jacobs had utilized both to his advantage, but still hadn't managed to get Bridget to agree to marry him. It proved how strong she really was.

The Lawman's Unwelcome Christmas Bride

It broke his heart to see the woman she was now. It made him even more determined to nurse her back to full health.

Wyatt gently lifted her from the chair as she slept, carrying her to bed. As he lay her down, she opened her eyes and screamed. "Bridget," he said quietly. "It's alright. It's me, Wyatt." She continued to scream. "It's Sheriff Hawkins," he said a little louder, and the screaming stopped.

It was clear to Wyatt it would take a lot of time for Bridget to heal. Far longer than he anticipated it would take to find and incarcerate Hugo Jacobs.

He sat on the side of the bed holding her hand until she settled again. Bridget's reaction made him think twice about the sleeping arrangements. He'd insisted she sleep in the spare room because of propriety. Except they were married, and there was no reason they couldn't share a bed. It wasn't like they were in love.

Bridget's fingers slipped from his hand as she rolled over. His heart felt hollow. As much as he didn't want to admit it, Wyatt missed holding her hand. His heart gave a little flutter when they touched, or he held her in his arms.

Wyatt mentally shook himself. Their marriage was not based on love. It was a marriage of convenience, orchestrated for one reason and one reason only – to give Bridget a new name in order to keep her safe.

Too bad Wyatt was beginning to have feelings for her. He needed to give himself a stern talking to, otherwise they would find themselves in deep trouble. The sort of trouble he vowed he wasn't interested in, and definitely didn't want.

Chapter Twelve

Bridget awoke only to find herself in a strange bed. It was wonderfully comfortable, and she didn't want to get out from under the luxurious bedding. Bridget wasn't sure how she got there, but surmised Wyatt had carried her from the sitting room last night.

Except…this wasn't the spare room, she was certain of it. She swung her legs out of the bed and sat on the side. The room wasn't at all familiar. She'd been in the spare room for a nap, and this wasn't it.

She glanced to the other side of the bed. It was empty, but had been slept in. The sheets were crinkled, and the pillow case was, too. Bridget reached across and grabbed the pillow, then put it to her nose. It had a masculine smell about it. Wyatt's smell.

Had she…? Bridget's heart pounded. She remembered little about the night before. She did recall dozing on a chair in the sitting room, but beyond that, she had no memory.

She threw the pillow aside, and her hand suddenly went to her chest. Did she sleep with Wyatt last night? It certainly appeared that way. The big question was had they consummated their marriage?

All the time she'd spent with Hugo, she'd fought him off. Bridget had kicked and screamed until he backed away. There was little privacy on the train. Hugo couldn't risk having the conductor investigate why there was screaming coming from their room. Her virtue had been saved as a result.

Bridget didn't know what to do. Should she ask Wyatt directly what happened, or wait to see if he brought it up? Her mind was still in confusion, and she wasn't sure what to do. Wyatt didn't seem the sort to take advantage of a person. Especially one who was in a difficult situation as Bridget was.

"Good morning," Wyatt said as he stood in the doorway.

Bridget's head snapped up, and she stared at him. "What happened last night?" she asked without thinking. "I don't recall coming to your bed."

His lips quivered and Bridget feared the worse. "After you screamed the place down in the spare room, I decided to move you in here." She scowled, and he must have realized what was going through her mind. His hands went up in front of himself. "Nothing happened, I promise. I wanted you closer, that's all." He ran a hand across his unshaven chin. "I didn't think about…I guess I didn't think about the consequences," he finally said.

"I guess you didn't," Bridget snapped before she could stop herself. She closed her eyes and shook her head. "I'm sorry, Wyatt. I didn't mean to snap. It's been horrific lately." Her blue eyes were flooded with tears when she opened them again. The last thing Bridget wanted was to have Wyatt see her tears. She was stronger than that.

He stepped toward the bed and sat beside her. Wyatt's arm went around her shoulder. "I understand," he said gently. "It's safer this way. The closer you are to me, the better it is."

Bridget gasped. "You don't think Hugo will break in here, do you? Into the sheriff's residence?" Bridget knew she was trembling, but had no control over the movement. She wasn't simply scared of Hugo finding her, she was downright terrified.

Wyatt tightened his grip. "He wouldn't be that stupid." It was a statement, but Bridget wondered if he was questioning the sanity of Hugo Jacobs and whether he would be so foolish as to break into a lawman's home.

If she had to guess, Bridget would say yes. Then a thought struck her. "If he knew I'd married, he might back off." Except Bridget wasn't so naïve as to think Hugo was that smart.

Wyatt studied her. "I will not use you as bait. This might not be a real marriage, but you are still my wife. I will protect you with my own life."

Bridget felt herself pale. She would never ask anyone to lay down their life for her. Especially someone as gallant as Wyatt. He had already put himself on the line when he went to find her few belongings. For all he knew, Hugo could have been out there waiting for Bridget. If he saw the sheriff instead, he wouldn't hesitate to kill him.

Wyatt stared into her face. "You're not going to swoon are you? I wouldn't know what to do except get the doc, and that's out of the question since I can't leave you alone." He rubbed at his chin again.

Bridget shook her head. "I won't, I promise." Except it was a promise she couldn't keep. She no longer had control over the way her body reacted. Doc Walker told her it would take a long time to recover, but she wished it wasn't so.

"I have breakfast ready. Let me help you up." He held both Bridget's hands and helped her to her feet. The contact with his skin was almost more than she could bear. Her fingers tingled, and it worried her. Did it mean she had no blood flowing to them? She certainly hoped not.

"I'll be fine," she said quietly, except Wyatt was having none of it. He clutched her hands and led her to the kitchen, where he sat her down. It was then

Bridget realized she was still wearing the gown she wore at their marriage ceremony. She felt like a pauper. Little money, no clothes, and no home of her own. It felt as though she was destitute, but in reality, she had money in the bank, a substantial inheritance, and a perfectly good home in her hometown of Helena. Except she couldn't risk going there in case Hugo found out she'd returned.

"I'm not destitute," she suddenly shouted, surprising even herself.

Wyatt stopped what he was doing and studied her, then sat down beside her at the table. "I know," he said gently. "That's the problem, isn't it? You are far from poor, and Hugo wants it all for himself." Wyatt pulled her to him and wrapped Bridget in his arms. For the first time for as long as she could remember, she felt wanted.

~*~

Staring at the pancakes Wyatt had made for breakfast, Bridget decided she needed to reach out and take one. Wyatt sat nearby, watching her every move. In the end, he put one on her plate. "Eat up before they get cold," he said, glancing down at his own food. He took a sip of his coffee, and Bridget stared at the mug of tea he'd made for her.

He lifted the maple syrup and offered her some. Bridget accepted. It looked inviting, it really did, but she had no compulsion to eat. Hugo really did her a lot of harm. What she had to do to fix it was the problem. Eating no longer came naturally. "Thank you," she whispered, then sipped her tea.

Wyatt staring at her wasn't helping, but she didn't blame him. He was looking out for her health. Finally, she picked up her knife and fork and cut a small piece of pancake. It felt as though it could melt in her mouth. "This is delicious," Bridget said.

He didn't answer, but grinned. Then Wyatt cut into his own food. He seemed rather pleased with himself.

As much as she didn't want to, Bridget decided she could get very used to Sheriff Hawkins being her husband.

Bridget was startled by a knock on the door. "Stay here," Wyatt told her as he took his gun from its holster. She heard the click of the door as it was unlocked, then the muffled sounds of talking. Soon afterwards, Wyatt returned to the kitchen carrying a large box. "Yesterday I asked Mrs. Walker to organize clothes and other essentials for you," he said matter-of-factly. "I told her to ensure there was plenty."

Bridget stood, but Wyatt insisted she wait until after they'd finished eating. He was right of course. She was more than a little excited about the prospect of having more than one gown to wear. She hoped there would be nightgowns and undergarments in the box as well. The anticipation she felt had Bridget eating everything on her plate, which seemed to please Wyatt.

Chapter Thirteen

Wyatt was thrilled to see Bridget finish her food. At first, he was annoyed Mrs. Walker had called so early, but it had turned out for the best. The older woman understood how his wife would be feeling without any clothes to call her own, so hurried to the mercantile the moment it opened. She would call around later to ensure the sizing was correct.

The thrill of rummaging through the box seemed to spur Bridget on. Wyatt did not care what had happened to get her to eat. He only cared she was getting good food in her belly. Each time she took a mouthful of food, her eyes strayed toward the box. He placed another pancake on her plate, covering it with maple syrup, and she didn't complain. "My mother made pancakes for breakfast," she said quietly, then took another mouthful. If it meant she would eat them each day, Wyatt would make them for her. At least this way he knew her health would have a chance of improving.

Wyatt was not domesticated. Far from it, but he did know how to make decent meals. He wasn't like a lot of the unattached men in town who lived on sausages and beans. He liked a good homecooked meal. It was then he realized he may need fresh supplies.

"Almost immediately after mother passed, Hugo pounced." Bridget's eyes went to her hands. "He knew no one would miss me. If he kidnapped me, there was no family to report I had disappeared." Her voice broke, and Wyatt felt a thud in his heart. How could anyone behave as Hugo Jacobs had done? He'd been in this job for a little over twenty years, and was still surprised at the inhumanity he dealt with on a regular basis.

Reaching across the table, Wyatt covered Bridget's hand with his own. She was petite, but with the loss of weight, she appeared tiny. She weighed almost nothing, he'd discovered the first time he'd carried her. "I'm sorry," he said, knowing his words meant little.

Her head bobbed, but Bridget said nothing. Tears swam in her eyes, but she blinked them back. Not only was she grieving the loss of her mother, but she also had to deal with the manipulative actions of Hugo Jacobs. The man was pure evil.

"I'll clean up while you explore what's in the box," Wyatt said, trying to change the subject. A smile came to Bridget's face and his heart fluttered. It pleased him to see her happy.

He carried the plates to the sink, but before he could even start washing, squeals of joy assaulted his ears. Wyatt couldn't help but turn to his wife. The happiness on her face was the best way he could think of to start the day.

Bridget held up one of the gowns in front of herself. "What do you think?" she asked as her cheeks colored. Why was she embarrassed? Because he had paid for her attire? She need not be – Bridget was his wife, and no matter what, he would look after her.

"It's beautiful. Mrs. Walker chose well," he said, stepping toward her. Bridget suddenly threw the gown back into the box, her happiness no longer visible. "What's wrong?" Wyatt asked.

Shaking her head, Bridget pursed her lips. He glanced down into the box, and then he saw it. Wyatt couldn't help but chuckle. "I'm your husband," he said, without adding the pretend part. "I am allowed to see your undergarments." Her cheeks turned a bright red, and it encouraged him to tease her further. "On or off," he said as he wiggled his eyebrows.

Wyatt couldn't help but laugh, but Bridget didn't see anything funny about it.

"Well, I never!" Bridget said, her embarrassment clear.

Wyatt stepped forward and wrapped her in his arms. "I was only joking," he whispered in her ear. "I will never take liberties with you." Her arms crept up and around his waist. She was so fragile, Wyatt barely knew they were there. Despite the fact, he reveled in knowing she trusted him. Leaning back slightly, he kissed her forehead. Moments later, Bridget leaned into him. The pair stayed that way for what seemed forever.

~*~

After a long hot bath, Bridget emerged from the small bathroom at the end of the hallway. She wore one of the new gowns Mrs. Walker had brought this morning. Bridget wore her hair down as it was still wet. "Do you mind if I sit beside the fire?" she asked. "My hair takes a long time to dry otherwise."

Of course he didn't mind, and directed her to the sitting room fire. That way he could stay by her side. Wyatt placed a pillow on the floor for his wife to sit on. She was all skin and bone, and he knew it would be uncomfortable for her otherwise.

As she reveled in the heat from the fire, he stared out the window. The ground was lightly covered by snow. It wasn't long until Christmas, and Wyatt knew he had to start planning for the big day. He was very aware this year might not be a day to celebrate. If Hugo was still on the loose, he would have to insist Bridget stay here in the sheriff's cottage with him.

"Is it snowing?" Her quiet voice pulled Wyatt out of his thoughts.

"It is. Everywhere you look, there's snow. Not enough to make a snowman, but enough to make it hazardous to walk around." Especially for Bridget. If she slipped, she might break a bone. He couldn't bear to see her injured further. "A few more days and the children will be out in this, having a great time."

She turned to him and smiled. "I would love to see them," she said, but Wyatt knew unless Hugo was behind bars, he couldn't risk letting her outside. As though she read his thoughts, Bridget sighed. Neither of them mentioned it again.

"There is room in the closet for your clothes," Wyatt said, trying to distract his wife. "When you're ready, let me know and I'll empty out one of the drawers for you."

She gazed at him. "Don't make changes on my account," she said quietly. "I won't be here long." Her words cut to his heart. Wyatt had become fond of Bridget, and was enjoying having her here. Until he'd brought her to live with him, albeit temporarily, Wyatt didn't know how lonely he was. Now he couldn't see himself living alone again.

Despite her desperate situation, Bridget had made his entire life better.

As he watched the townsfolk go about their business, Wyatt noticed a stranger. Someone he'd never seen before. He helped Bridget to her feet, and had her identify the man. Was it Hugo? His heart pounded in the belief he'd found her so quickly.

"It's not Hugo," she said quietly. "The man you pointed out is tall and muscular. Hugo isn't much taller than me, and is wiry. You can almost knock him over with a feather."

Much like Bridget, Wyatt thought, but didn't say the words out loud. "Thank you," he said, then assisted her to sit by the fire again. He closed the window coverings and sat down on one of the comfortable chairs. "I should start lunch," he said. "How do you feel about vegetable soup?"

"It sounds delicious," she said, even though Wyatt already knew she wouldn't eat much. He would make biscuits too, since Bridget seemed to enjoy them.

He continued to sit in the comfortable chair, waiting for her hair to dry. As much as he was sure Bridget was safe here in the sitting room, even without him, Wyatt refused to take the risk. Bridget was scared and vulnerable, and he wouldn't leave her alone. Not even for a few minutes while he prepared the vegetables for lunch. If it meant they ate later than normal, so be it. Her safety and well-being was far more important.

Chapter Fourteen

Bridget's hair was now dry, but she didn't want to move. It was so warm and cozy next to the fire, but she did need to brush her hair, and put it up. Wyatt had treated her so kindly, and she thought about a way to repay him. Although he'd said it was his job to protect her, Wyatt had gone beyond what was expected of a sheriff.

For one, he didn't have to marry her. Bridget didn't care about propriety. Besides, hadn't she'd been locked in a room with Hugo for an unbearable amount of time? Propriety meant nothing to her. Only she was too weak to argue. Not with the doc, his wife, or with Wyatt. Once the danger was over, they would seek an annulment. That was the agreement.

What if she didn't want an annulment? What would happen then?

She'd become comfortable with Wyatt. More than comfortable if she was honest with herself. It was like she'd known him all her life. The truth was, Bridget felt far more comfortable around Wyatt than she did with any of the men she'd know since she was a child. They had tried to win her heart and her inheritance, but their advances hadn't worked.

It wasn't that she didn't like any of them. It was simply the fact Bridget knew they were after her money. Several she hadn't seen since she left school, which was a long time ago. She wasn't quite there yet, but she was steaming toward forty. Who would want a bride of her age? She may not even be able to bear children. Most men seemed to want a family. An heir to take over their ranch or whatever business they had.

Of course, Bridget wanted a family, too, but believed that ship had sailed long ago. It was a pity. Bridget had always believed she would make an excellent mother. Still, she could be wrong.

As she tried to bring herself to her feet, Bridget stumbled. Wyatt was by her side before she could fall. "Here, let me help," he said taking hold of both her hands.

Bridget glanced up at his face. He was genuinely concerned for her. It was refreshing to find someone who didn't want her only for her money. "I could have got up by myself," she snapped, then thought the better of it. Wyatt was not Hugo. There was only one reason Hugo helped her at any point, and that was to ensure she was able to say *I do* in front of a preacher.

It was too late for that now. Hugo would be hugely disappointed when he found out she was already married. "Sorry," she said quietly. "I know you were only trying to help."

Wyatt stared at her for longer than felt comfortable. She squirmed under his watchful eyes. "I know," he said, then lifted her and carried Bridget to a chair. "Let me rebandage your sprained ankle.

As much as she didn't want to be treated like an invalid, Bridget couldn't deny she enjoyed being in Wyatt's arms. It didn't only make her feel safe; there was something more. What it was, Bridget didn't know. The more she thought about it, the harder it became to fathom what it might be. "I need to brush my hair," she said quietly once he'd seated her. "Mrs. Walker thought of everything – there's a hair brush in the boxes of goodies she brought over this morning. Since mine never did resurface."

"Shall I fetch it?" Wyatt asked. Bridget wondered if he would be embarrassed going through the unmentionables to get to the brush.

"Only if you want to," she said firmly, as though she was trying to warn Wyatt of what he might find. He might not have ever been married before, but surely he'd dealt with women's undergarments before.

"Of course," he said, then disappeared into the kitchen.

The thought made her wonder. He was a true gentleman, there was no doubt in her mind. Perhaps he hadn't had such dealings. Too late now, he was already in the kitchen looking for the hair brush. Bridget felt the heat rise in her cheeks. She hoped he didn't come back wearing that grin of his. If she did, she would know for sure he'd come across her unmentionables.

Sure enough, when he reentered the sitting room, he had a silly grin on his face. Instead of being embarrassed as Bridget suspected she would be, she felt mild irritation. She met his grin with a scowl. His grin quickly disappeared.

Much to her surprise, Wyatt offered to brush Bridget's hair. It was close to dry so shouldn't be too difficult for him to manage. When she was a young girl, her mother would brush her hair. It was a ritual with them – after her bath, and her hair was dry, Bridget would sit on the floor while her mother sat behind her on a chair.

Not that it was necessary, but often it took an hour or more. Bridget always suspected it didn't need to take that long. Her theory was her mother used the hair brushing sessions to get closer to her daughter.

Back then, they had servants for everything. It meant Mother was not her main carer. Not in the way other mothers were with their children. It was a special time for the pair, and Bridget didn't want it to ever stop.

They continued the ritual even when Bridget was an adult, and didn't stop until her mother was too ill to participate in what had become special to both of them.

Wyatt brushed her hair with what seemed to be practiced precision. Not once was he heavy handed. Nor did he drag her head back at any point. "You've done this before," she said matter-of-factly.

She heard him chuckle. "It fell on me to brush my younger sister's hair." He chuckled again. "I guess you weren't expecting that."

It was the last thing on Bridget's mind. She thought Wyatt would be naïve to such things, but he'd proven her wrong. "Do you see her?" she asked, then thought the better of it. "Sorry, it's not my business."

"It's fine," he said. "When Mary-Ann married and moved interstate, we lost touch." Bridget heard the regret in his voice, and it cut right to her heart. "We exchanged letters for the first few years, but then the letters stopped."

"You didn't check up on her?" she said, her voice accusing. "Do you even know if she's still alive?"

"I…" Wyatt stumbled at her harsh words. He stopped brushing her hair, and his hand went to her shoulder. "I did check on her. She died in child birth, along with her baby."

The memory made him sad, she could tell. "I'm sorry," Bridget said quietly. "It wasn't my place to ask." She wondered why Mary-Ann's husband hadn't notified her brother about what happened.

"Her husband was also her doctor. He blamed himself, according to the sheriff, and turned to drink. Within days he was trampled by a horse after one particularly bad drinking session. The local sheriff contacted me to advise it was fatal," Wyatt said, his voice breaking. "Thankfully, they had no other children."

Bridget reached around and covered Wyatt's hand with her own. He suddenly pulled his hand away and began to brush her hair again. This was the most information she knew about her husband. Bridget wondered if he would tell her more the longer they were together.

Except she knew it wouldn't happen. The moment Hugo was arrested, their marriage would be annulled.

Chapter Fifteen

Wyatt couldn't believe how much talking about his sister's death affected him. It wasn't like it was recent – she died many years ago now. Despite not seeing her for some time before her death, he still missed her.

Bridget was able to get him to talk about things he had no wish to discuss. She had her own problems, yet she easily convinced him to talk about his. It was concerning to Wyatt. He wasn't the sort to air his dirty laundry, as the saying went.

His heart thudded merely thinking about Mary-Ann. She had died needlessly in his eyes. She had wanted a baby for many years. When she finally fell pregnant there were more complications than he could remember. Her doctor husband, unable to save his wife or their baby, blamed himself for their demise. Wyatt would never have placed blame on him.

Still, his heart continued to thud. Bridget's hand covering his had been comforting. Except Wyatt knew he couldn't get close to his *wife*. The moment Hugo Jacobs was behind bars, she would be free to do whatever she wanted to do. The mere thought of her leaving cut deep to his heart.

As he continued to brush her hair, thoughts of his sister lingered. Wyatt knew he should have made the time to visit Mary-Ann and her husband. Except he had a job to do, and the townsfolk expected their sheriff to be available at all times. What they were thinking now made him wonder.

Still, it had to be done. He could send out a call for the marshals to come to Halliwell Junction, but that would likely scare the man away. Jacobs wasn't a high profile criminal, he was more a petty thief. Up until he kidnapped Bridget, anyway. It meant the marshals wouldn't have much interest in helping Wyatt.

Which also meant he had to rely on his own skills and those of his deputies. Deputy Jonah Simpson was reliable. Of that, Wyatt was certain. He'd been deputy since before Wyatt arrived. While he didn't want the responsibility of sheriff, he happily carried out his deputy duties. His second deputy was fairly new to the job. Andrew Hartwick wasn't from Halliwell Junction. He was a city slicker. Heck, he could barely ride a horse!

Wyatt still couldn't work out why Hartwick had been posted here, but was working on sorting out the kinks. He would make a decent deputy out of him yet. When Wyatt retired, which was a long way off, he wanted to know the town was placed in capable hands.

He sighed. These thoughts that were running unbidden through his mind had to stop. Before he married Bridget Spencer, he had no such thoughts. What was it about her that forced his mind to ramble?

"Thank you," Bridget said, breaking into his reflections.

She turned around to face him, and Wyatt gasped. He saw her properly for the first time. Not only was her red hair beautiful now it had been washed, but Bridget herself appeared different. She was still pale and drawn, and what would have been once rosy lips were almost devoid of color. When he gazed into her sky blue eyes, his heart fluttered. For no other reason than he'd finally seen the real person, not only the woman who needed protecting.

She endeavored to stand up, but with her ankle sprained and bandaged, it was difficult. "Let me help," he said, and didn't wait for her answer. Wyatt stood, and taking both her small hands, helped Bridget to her feet. She gazed up into his face as he stared down into hers.

Not for the first time, Wyatt felt a connection between them. It wasn't the fact he'd rescued her. He'd dismissed the conclusion long ago. There was something more, but he wasn't sure what. It felt almost like magic. As though an unnatural force was pulling them together.

He continued to stare at her, and Bridget studied him. Suddenly she pulled her hands out of his grip and put them around him. She leaned against his chest, and stayed there for a very long time. Wyatt knew he should put a stop to it, but didn't have the heart.

Besides, he liked it, and had no intention of telling her otherwise. His heart pounded faster than it ever had before, and he was sure there would be a reason for it. Other than a heart attack, that was, something he was certain wasn't the case.

His arms went up around his wife, and she didn't complain. As he pulled her closer still, she seemed to snuggle into him. How long they stayed like that, Wyatt didn't know.

What he did know was he didn't want to let her go. When their annulment was processed, Wyatt wasn't sure how he would survive.

Bridget Hawkins, his pretend wife, had become more than a stranger he was protecting.

~*~

Wyatt pulled all the window coverings closed. It was almost dark outside, and he didn't want anyone to be able to see inside. According to Deputy Simpson, there were no strangers in town. The man he'd seen earlier was a traveler, trying to sell his wares. He'd since left.

The deputy promised to give Wyatt updates every day. Wyatt refused to leave the sheriff's cottage and leave Bridget alone. It wasn't worth the risk.

However, they had a bigger problem. Bridget was the only person in town who knew what Hugo Jacobs looked like. There were no wanted posters that showed his likeness, and it caused a dilemma. How would they know when the criminal arrived in town if no one knew it was him?

After voicing his concerns to his deputy earlier in the day, Bridget requested paper and a pencil. Wyatt watched as she sketched out a man's image. "I guess all those art lessons didn't go to waste," she said, sarcasm dripping from every word. "My father insisted I go to one of those finishing schools. I told him there was little value in sending me there, but he wouldn't have it," Bridget said as she handed over the drawing. "That's Hugo Jacobs. He is short and scrawny, and has been, at times, mistaken for a teenager." Her lips curled at the last words, but Wyatt knew she wasn't kidding. "He tried desperately for me to marry him while mother was still alive. My skin crawled simply having him nearby." She shuddered then, and Wyatt realized the mere thought of the man repulsed her.

His hand went to her shoulder, and he felt the shiver that ran through her. He wanted to pull Bridget to her feet and hold her tight. Except he couldn't do that with his deputy standing nearby.

Instead, he studied the image of the fugitive. "Take it to the sheriff's office," Wyatt told Deputy Simpson. "His image is ingrained in my mind. Believe me when I say I will never forget that face." His last words were said on a snarl, which was not his intention. Hatred had filled him, and the realization shocked Wyatt. He was not one to feel such a strong emotion.

It wasn't like he knew Bridget. Not really.

They'd only recently met. If he analyzed his actions, he knew there would be confirmation that he was developing feelings for his make-believe wife. When she was treated poorly, it cut to his heart.

Wyatt knew when he came face to face with Hugo Jacobs he would have to keep his emotions tightly in control.

Chapter Sixteen

Bridget was shocked to hear the emotion in Wyatt's voice. From the moment they'd met, he had been all business. As she would expect. Now things were different, and she wasn't sure why.

He'd all but snarled those last words, and it made her hope Wyatt wasn't the one to arrest Hugo. Not for Hugo's sake, she didn't care about him at all, but for her husband's.

Keeping things professional was already becoming a challenge. At least for Bridget. Although there were clues here and there Wyatt might be feeling the same way. Except Bridget knew it was inevitable many women fell for their protectors. The reverse was also true.

Especially when they were forced into close proximity as was the case here. Hopefully it would only be a few more days and she would be free to go wherever she wanted. Bridget didn't know how long it took to process an annulment, so she might have to stay in Halliwell Junction longer than anticipated.

"Can I help prepare supper?" she asked, trying to keep things on a more friendly basis. The more they spoke about Hugo, the more charged the air between them seemed to get.

Wyatt stared at her. "You are meant to have your foot up," he said, gazing at her. "Doc Walker will have my hide if you don't do the right thing."

His words made her smile. What could the older man do to the sheriff? Not much, she surmised. Bridget chuckled. The image in her mind was too farfetched to even explain.

"Come on," he said, gesturing her into the sitting room. "Sit down. Wyatt glanced around the room and found the pillow Bridget had used earlier. He pulled a side table closer and reached for Bridget's leg.

Then he hesitated. Of course they were married, and it was as though he suddenly realized the fact. He hitched her skirts up slightly, and gripped her leg gently, placing it on the pillow.

Then he glanced at her. Was Wyatt waiting for her to call him out on lifting her skirts? Probably. Did she care he'd done so? A little, but there was a reason for his actions. Besides, as Bridget kept reminding herself, they were married.

It might be only for show, a marriage of convenience until all this nonsense with Hugo was over, but they were legally husband and wife. No one could tell them otherwise.

Bridget wasn't sure how she felt about that. Right now though, apart from Hugo kidnapping and torturing her, Bridget was happy right where she was.

Wyatt continued to stare. It made Bridget feel a little uncomfortable, although his gaze wasn't with bad intent. He seemed to be assessing her. Such as you'd expect a sheriff to do. "Are you comfortable?" he finally asked, his eyes searching her face.

"Not really," she replied. "It's the best it can be though." And it was. Sticking ones leg out and upwards did not come naturally. Nor was it the most comfortable position to be in. Bridget couldn't wait for her time in purgatory to end. In other words, she wouldn't be completely happy until the bandage came off.

Wyatt appeared pained. "If you prefer, I can set you up on the bed. It may be more comfortable?"

Or it may not, she silently told herself. This certainly wasn't exactly blissful, but she could endure it a little longer. Bridget shook her head. "At least in here I have company." She smiled briefly, trying to reassure Wyatt she would be fine.

She glanced out the window, as much as she could from where she sat. "Oh, it's snowing," she said, her heart fluttering. "I used to love building snowmen when I was a child."

Wyatt came to sit beside her. "I did too. Perhaps one day we will have children who enjoy it too." Bridget was shocked by his words. Did he expect they would have children together? It was not something she expected him to say. "I didn't mean… That is…" He stumbled over his words then, finally shrugging his shoulders and giving up. "I'm making coffee. Do you want tea?" he asked over his shoulder as he headed toward the kitchen.

"Thank you, yes," she called as he disappeared into the other room.

It wasn't long before Wyatt appeared again, with two mugs and a plate of cookies. "I didn't mean to imply," his cheeks reddened, and it took all her effort not to giggle. Except laughing at his discomfort would be rude.

"It's fine," Bridget said as she reached for the mug of hot tea. She wasn't really hungry, but Wyatt seemed keen for her to take a cookie. He shoved the plate toward her several times until she gave in. "Thank you," she said, nibbling the cookie.

Wyatt sat down beside her, and helped himself to a cookie. "Mrs. Walker brought these for us," he said, taking a large bite. "She's an excellent cook."

Bridget nibbled again as she felt Wyatt's eyes on her. Was he monitoring how much she ate, or was it simply Bridget's imagination? She decided it was a little of both. Whenever they ate, his eyes drifted her way. She was certain it was with intent. Doc Walker told Wyatt he needed to ensure she ate. She was trying, she truly was, but Hugo had starved her for too long, which made it difficult to stomach anything. A little at a time, that was all she could manage.

An image of her tormentor came into Bridget's mind, and she gasped. The mug of tea almost slipped from her hands, but Wyatt was there to ensure she wasn't burned.

"What happened?" he asked. "Are you alright?" He seemed genuinely concerned about her well being.

"I saw Hugo," she whispered. Wyatt dashed to the window and glanced out. "Not out there. In my mind." Now Bridget was confused. Was Hugo there in the flesh, or did she merely see a vision of him? "At least I think it was in my mind."

Wyatt studied the few people that lingered outside in the cold and the snow. "I don't see anyone that resembles the image you drew." He continued to stare out the window, and that bothered Bridget.

Was Hugo here, or not? Either way, she needed to know. Safe in the knowledge he wasn't in town had

Bridget relaxing. Now there was a possibility he was in Halliwell Junction, and it had her on edge.

Wyatt glanced over his shoulder at her. He quickly closed the window coverings and sat down beside her. "I don't believe he's in town. It doesn't mean my guard will be down. Tonight and every night until we apprehend Hugo Jacobs, you will sleep in the master bedroom. I need to be certain you are safe," he said. Wyatt reached for her hand and a shiver went down her spine.

Bridget was in trouble. Big trouble. She was becoming more enamored with her make-believe husband with every passing moment.

It was not how this was supposed to work.

Chapter Seventeen

Wyatt could not believe he'd invited Bridget into his bed. Temptation wriggled closer each time she spoke, and with every touch.

They were both adults, and they would control their feelings. Of course they would. Besides, because Wyatt had feelings for Bridget did not mean she had any such feelings for him. She was good at keeping her emotions intact, and until recently, Wyatt believed he did too.

Except now he only had to be near to her, and he was more aware of Bridget than he had any right to be. He wanted to pull her close against him and hold her tight. Make all her problems disappear. If only it was as easy as closing the window coverings as he'd done earlier.

He didn't for one minute believe she'd seen Hugo Jacobs out there. How would he know Bridget was in the sheriff's cottage? Almost no one had that information, except a privileged few, and they wouldn't pass that information on. Not to anyone. Especially a stranger.

Besides, Wyatt had studied the few people who were out and about, and he was certain Jacobs wasn't one of them.

Unless he was in disguise.

It wasn't a possibility Wyatt had contemplated before, but Jacobs was a criminal with deceitful intent. He would do anything to get his hands on Bridget's money. Only he was too late.

It was in this moment of clarity Wyatt realized the situation he was now in. Since marrying Bridget *he* was the one to inherit all that money. Except he didn't want it.

If it came down to a choice – Bridget or her money – he would choose his wife. Money had never meant much to Wyatt. He earned enough money to live comfortably, and had also managed to put a little away each month.

One day, when he was ready to settle down, Wyatt would buy a ranch, not a big rambling one, but one small enough he could manage with only one or two workers at most. A place that was reasonably close to Halliwell Junction would suit him perfectly. His biggest joy would be to settle down there with the woman he loved, and eventually the pair would have children of their own.

His eyes wandered to Bridget. Would she be the woman he settled down with? Wyatt shook himself mentally. His foolish thoughts needed to stop right now.

His marriage with Bridget was short term, and only for show. The moment Hugo Jacobs was arrested, they would go before a judge and have their marriage annulled.

Wyatt couldn't work out why the thought left him feeling miserable.

~*~

Snow was falling far heavier now, and it gave Wyatt a sense of warmth. He wasn't sure why it was the case when it was cold – both inside and out. He'd refueled the fire earlier in the evening, and now supper was over, he was pleased he had. The sitting room was warm and cozy, just the way he liked it.

Deputy Simpson had called in to give Wyatt an update. There was nothing to report. As far as the deputy could tell, Jacobs was not in town. Wyatt's concern was in the fact no one knew for sure. It made him wonder how long it had taken Jacobs to realize Bridget was missing. He would backtrack from there, stopping at every town along the way.

It would not be long before Hugo Jacobs arrived at Halliwell Junction. Waiting around for trains to arrive would not be Jacobs style. Wyatt knew the type – he would steal a horse instead of being inconvenienced.

His heart thudded. Despite the snow and the cold, Hugo Jacobs was on a mission. His mission was to steal Bridget's inheritance then dispose of her. Without understanding why, Wyatt felt hollow. There was something terribly wrong but he couldn't put his finger on it.

Glancing across at Bridget had his heart fluttering. Warmth flooded him, but Wyatt fought the feelings. He was not falling in love with his make-believe wife. He simply wouldn't allow himself to do so.

Except he already had. She held a mug of tea in her petite hands. He knew from the start she was fragile. Jacobs had done that to her. Even though Wyatt didn't know her before she arrived, he was certain Bridget was not delicate in the same way she was now. This was all Hugo Jacobs doing.

He had starved her, deprived her of sleep, and who knew what else. His heart thudded. If Jacobs laid a hand on his wife, he would…

Wyatt had to stop overthinking everything. Bridget told him what Jacobs had done. She was forthcoming in that regard. He peeked behind the curtains and glanced about. It seemed to be quiet outside, and he couldn't see anyone wandering about. As it should be with this weather.

What he did see was a large Christmas tree outside the mercantile. He knew Christmas was coming up, but he'd been so busy with caring for Bridget, it hadn't crossed his mind again.

"Are you alright?" Bridget's voice cut through his mindless internal rambling.

He spun around so quickly, he almost tumbled to the floor. "Never better," he lied as he restored his footing. "How are you feeling?"

She smiled briefly, and Wyatt understood she'd seen right through him. "I hope Doc Walker is still coming tomorrow. I can't wait to have this bandage removed." She sighed then, and Wyatt felt for her. She didn't seem like the type of woman to sit aside while there were tasks to be done.

He sat beside her, and reached for his coffee. Studying Bridget, he could see a marked difference from when she arrived to now. She was still thin, still frail, but she was slowly filling out. It would take weeks, if not months, for her to be restored to full health.

Wyatt would be there for her during that process, and afterwards. Of course he would.

Except…

By then, their marriage would be annulled. No doubt Bridget would be back in her own home in Helena. Jacobs would be incarcerated, or perhaps even hanged. She wouldn't need Wyatt's protection any more.

After all, that's what this was all about. He'd known it from the start, but only now the reality had hit. His wife, who was beautiful in many ways, would no longer be his wife. The very thought was like a dagger thrust to his heart.

Chapter Eighteen

Bridget was convinced she'd seen Hugo outside the window of the sitting room. Except Wyatt had seen no such person. In fact, he'd stated no one was nearby. How could that be?

The only explanation was her imagination was getting away with her. She had never been a person to exaggerate or even to embellish the truth. She hadn't done it this time either. Not to her knowledge anyway.

She should be pleased with the deputy's report. No sightings of Hugo Jacobs in town. Except no one knew where he was. Bridget knew it was inevitable he would eventually turn up. Hugo was like a dog with a bone – what he deemed to be his, in this case, Bridget, or more likely her inheritance – he would fight until the end to get it.

A shiver went down her spine. He was here in Halliwell Junction. Bridget was certain he was. He had to take shelter somewhere, and from what she'd been told, the saloon was the only place where he could get a room. Hugo was frugal with his money, but in this case, she was sure he would be prepared to spend money to get his hands on her inheritance.

She shivered again.

Bridget felt eyes on her, but she knew it wasn't Hugo. She gingerly glanced up to see Wyatt staring at her. "What is it?" he demanded, although his voice was low.

"I…I sense Hugo is in town," she said, then trembled. Her hands were shaking, along with her entire body.

Wyatt sat down beside her and put his arm around her shoulders. "He won't get anywhere near you. It's a promise."

Studying his face, Bridget could see the sincerity, and nodded. She still had her reservations, but she knew Wyatt to be trustworthy. He was good at his job and had promised he would keep her safe.

No matter her vow to keep her distance, Bridget sank into him. Wyatt lifted his free hand and caressed her cheek. She didn't complain. She'd come to care for Wyatt, all the time knowing she shouldn't. The moment Hugo was arrested, their marriage would be annulled.

Her heart shattered. All her adult life, Bridget was a loner. She had no thought of marriage, despite her father pushing her toward unsuitable men. After

Father died, Mother took over, but was more receptive to her wishes.

Bridget's father had worked hard to build a thriving business. Within days of his death, men she had not seen since their school days began to call. They disguised their visits as passing on their condolences, but Bridget saw right through them. A short time later they returned and expressed their wish to court her.

Of course they did. Father had amassed a fortune. Enough to ensure her *suitors* would never have to work again. He also left her with a monthly allowance to guarantee Bridget could continue her charitable work and never need to find a job.

Hugo was the first to visit. He was like a vulture, hovering above its prey, then pouncing the moment it was dead. He'd even had the audacity to call around while Father was dying. He'd ingratiated himself with her parents, but Bridget saw right through him. It made her realize Hugo had learned the conditions of her father's will. She would not receive anything except her allowance until she married.

How Hugo found out, she had no idea, but it put her in grave danger, as had been proven.

She snuggled into Wyatt's chest. Bridget didn't want to think about Hugo, or the fact he was willing to murder her to get hold of her father's money.

What she couldn't understand was how he hadn't discovered she was now married.

"We kept it quiet," Wyatt told her.

Had she spoken out loud? Bridget felt as though she was losing her mind. And no wonder, given what she'd been through with Hugo. "Perhaps you shouldn't have," she answered, her mind wandering all over the place. "If Hugo knows I'm married, he might give up."

"Except he may disappear and you will be forever looking over your shoulder." Wyatt stared down into her face with sad eyes. "No, this way he will continue to look for you, and we'll apprehend him."

"I'm locked in here, in the sheriff's cottage. He won't know I'm even in town."

Wyatt frowned. Bridget knew she was right, but what could they do about it? Hugo was the type to ignore the reality and drag her off to a preacher to marry him anyway.

It got her mind to thinking. Whether Wyatt would go along with the idea, she couldn't be sure.

~*~

"Absolutely not!" Wyatt was fuming, as Bridget knew he would be. "I will not put your life at risk in order to catch Hugo Jacobs." His eyes seemed to turn a darker shade of blue, but perhaps it was merely her imagination.

"You said it yourself – Hugo doesn't know I'm here. With it being the case, he will never come to Halliwell Junction, and therefore he will never be caught."

Wyatt sighed. He stood then paced the room, his hands fisted. He shook his head as if reiterating to Bridget it wasn't going to happen. "He's dangerous, you know that already, so why would you even suggest it?"

Bridget sat upright and straightened her shoulders. "Because I know it will work. My plan will lure him here. Once he's in town, you and your deputies can pounce and arrest him."

It was the perfect plan, and Wyatt knew it. Why he wouldn't agree, Bridget had no idea. "I can't stay locked away forever. We both need to reclaim our lives."

It was the truth, and Wyatt couldn't deny it. Neither of them was content at being prisoners in the sheriff's cottage. Although from her perspective, Bridget had enjoyed getting to know the sheriff. Even if he didn't feel the same way.

Chapter Nineteen

Wyatt couldn't believe Bridget had even suggested it. Her plan could work, he was certain. However, it would put her in grave danger. He had no doubt Hugo Jacobs would fall for what she had in store. The man was greedy, and that was the truth of it.

Men like Jacobs wanted the easy way out. When he found out about Bridget's inheritance, the man had evidently planned exactly how he intended to get his hands on it. Right down to eliminating Bridget the moment the inheritance went through to his bank account.

Wyatt shuddered at the very thought.

Of course, Bridget's plan would work. From what he'd learned of Jacobs, he was fool enough to fall for it. Except he had to get the cooperation of a few other people. Surely it wouldn't be that hard.

Bridget stood unsteadily, and he moved next to her. Without thinking, his arms went around her. Leaning in, she rested her head against his chest. "I know you don't like the idea, but it will work. I guarantee it." She stared up at him, and Wyatt gazed into her blue eyes. He brushed her flaming red hair back off her face, and simply studied her.

He licked his lips, then leaned into his make-believe wife. Her lips were poised perfectly for him to kiss her. She didn't pull away, and he took that as consent. He lightly brushed his lips across hers, then leaned back. Her eyes seemed to sparkle, but she didn't say a word. Instead, she reached up and pulled him back down.

Back to her lips. Except this time *she* kissed *him*. There were no regrets on Wyatt's part, but when it was all said and done, would Bridget have regrets? He couldn't help but wonder.

The more he thought about it, the more Wyatt knew he'd done the wrong thing. She was vulnerable, and he had no right to take advantage of her like this.

"Is there a problem?" Her words were barely above a whisper.

He straightened up and stepped away. "I'm supposed to be protecting you. Seducing you is not appropriate," he said firmly. Her jaw dropped and she stared at him. "I'm making coffee. Tea for you?" he asked, but she didn't answer. Instead, Bridget continued to stare.

Finally, Bridget nodded. She snatched up the crutches and followed him into the kitchen. "I've decided to follow through with my plan," she said boldly.

Wyatt's heart hammered. She would be putting herself at risk. High risk. He had refused her suggestion because of the danger to herself, but knew he couldn't stop her. He had absolutely no control over his pretend wife. Now she was feeling somewhat better, she was showing her bossy side.

It was all he could do to stop himself grinning.

She glared at him. "What?" she demanded. "What are you smiling about?"

Wyatt didn't mean to smile. In fact he thought he had his lips under control. Then again, perhaps not, since he'd kissed his charge. They might be married, but it wasn't real, and he needed to remember the fact.

He didn't answer, and was certain he had a silly grin on his face now. "Here's your tea," he said, placing it on the table. Then turned back to add some cookies to a plate. He carried them, along with his mug of coffee, to the table. "Let's talk about this some more," Wyatt said.

The shocked expression on her face was priceless. He reminded Bridget just because he wanted to discuss it, didn't mean the plan would go ahead.

~*~

The arrangements were made, and everything was in place. Now to wait.

As a lawman, Wyatt was used to waiting. To being patient in order to catch the bad guys. This case was different. His aim was to catch the man who wanted to kill his wife.

"That feels so much better. Thanks, Doc," Bridget said as Doc Walker removed the bandage and inspected her ankle.

The doctor stood up. "There seems to be no permanent damage, which is the best outcome we could have hoped for." He rubbed a hand across the back of his neck. "Promise me something," he said sternly, staring down at her. "No more jumping out of trains." He chuckled then. It wasn't something the doc often did, and it made Wyatt chuckle along with him.

"I will keep an eye on her, I promise," Wyatt said firmly. At least while they were married. After that, when Bridget returned to her old life, he would have no control whatsoever. By then, Jacobs would be behind bars, and Wyatt would have no valid reason to keep her here.

The mere thought of losing her cut right to his heart. Wyatt knew he had no control over Bridget, not know and not ever. She went along with being at the cottage with him for her own safety. What she'd done to draw Hugo Jacobs to Halliwell Junction was foolish. There was no other way to put it.

But by gosh, Wyatt knew it would work.

They said their goodbyes to Doc Walker and he retreated. He was aware of the plan, and would play a part in it. Like Wyatt, he had his reservations.

Using Bridget as bait…Wyatt didn't want to think about the consequences. What if it all went awry? He shook himself mentally. It was foolish to agree, although she'd given him no choice. It wasn't so much he agreed, but Bridget told Wyatt no matter if he agreed or not, she was going through with the plan.

It was already set in motion, and there was nothing he could do about it. "How does your ankle feel now the bandage is off?" Wyatt asked, trying to get the dread out of his mind. All he could think about was Jacobs coming to town, seeking her out, and killing her.

Not that the man would get anywhere near Bridget. She was under Wyatt's watchful eye all day and all night. And would continue to be until Jacobs was behind bars.

He'd made good on his word she would sleep with him. It had been excruciating having her sleep beside him each night. Bridget was reluctant at first, but quickly got used to it. Even when she awoke to his arm across her body.

Wyatt knew he could get very used to having her in his bed. Only he wanted their marriage to be real now.

Chapter Twenty

Today was the day.

At least Bridget hoped it was. The *Halliwell Times* was distributed late yesterday, and would be in the hands of readers by now.

Do You Know This Woman?

The heading was bold and enticing. Exactly as Bridget wanted it to be. Wyatt watched over her shoulder.

Bridget was shocked at how thin and drawn she appeared in the photograph, but it was for the better.

Do You Know This Amnesia Victim? the subheading read. The story was given front page news. It hadn't taken a lot of convincing the editor of the newspaper to agree to running the article when he heard the story. The parts he wanted to publish couldn't be included, but Bridget promised to give him an exclusive interview once Hugo was captured.

She could see the headline now – *Heiress Held Captive by Deranged Man*

It was the truth, and she couldn't get away from it. Instead of wallowing in self-pity, Bridget needed to concentrate on trapping Hugo.

The plan was simple – the article would draw Hugo to Halliwell Junction. Bridget was convinced Hugo would claim she was his wife. Since Bridget supposedly had no memory of who she was, how could anyone challenge him?

It was a simple plan, but one she knew would work.

Wyatt on the other hand was not happy. He agreed the set-up would work, but did not like the dangerous aspects of Bridget putting herself on the front page of the newspaper for all to see. Since the *Halliwell Times* was only distributed in the local county, there was no chance anyone in Helena would see the article. Therefore, it couldn't destabilize their idea.

She hadn't been able to sleep, Bridget was so nervous. It wasn't surprising. Wyatt also stayed awake most of the night. The pair were up early, and had breakfast. Everything was ready to go. All they needed now was for Hugo to turn up as planned.

Despite the cold and the snow, Bridget knew he would arrive sooner than later. She also knew Hugo would use their train tickets as proof he was her husband. He'd bought the tickets as Mr. Hugo Jacobs and Mrs. Bridget Jacobs.

No one questioned the validity of their marriage despite locals knowing Bridget wasn't married. They simply accepted whatever Hugo said. Slipping the ticket seller a *tip* surely helped.

The moment the pair were ready, Bridget and Wyatt headed toward the doctor's office. The article mentioned the confused woman was being cared for there. It was the perfect ruse – who would suspect the local doctor to be in cahoots with the sheriff? Certainly not Hugo who only had his own purpose in mind.

Her heart pounded at the realization the end of her ordeal could be near. The fact Wyatt would be there with her was the one thing keeping Bridget calm. Before this torment occurred, she could and did endure anything. She had always been strong in body and in mind.

Hugo had reduced her to a mere shadow of herself.

She wasn't a vengeful person, but Bridget was determined Hugo would pay for what he'd done. Not only for herself, but for any future victims he might scheme to deceive.

The moment they arrived at the doctor's office, everything was put into play. Wyatt had arrived not as a sheriff but as a doctor. The doctor's wife, Hilda Walker, left for the day as requested by the sheriff. He had no intention of putting her in danger.

The deputies had their eyes on the place, and would keep doing so until Hugo Jacobs arrived.

Wyatt wanted to have him claim Bridget as his wife before he arrested the man. It wasn't like he didn't have enough to arrest him already, but the more charges against him the better. Kidnap and torture were bad enough, but fraud for financial gain put his crimes into a whole new level.

Bridget was taken into the infirmary where she would be seen as the woman with amnesia. Wyatt was posing as a doctor. Hugo wouldn't know any different. When the time was right, Wyatt would pounce.

Wyatt, Bridget, and Doc Walker sat sipping hot beverages. Bridget's hands shook, and Wyatt covered them, allowing her to drink her tea. Except that wasn't all he did. His touch sent a shiver cascading from her hands, all the way up her arm.

She decided to ignore it. Except she couldn't.

Wyatt stared into her eyes. "Are you alright?" he whispered.

Bridget nodded. "As much as I can be," she said quietly. "If Hugo saw the article, he'll be here today. He wouldn't wait any longer than necessary.

Wyatt kept his hands covering hers, and for Bridget, it was the reassurance she needed. There was a knock at the door, and Doc Walker gingerly left the room and opened the door. When he returned, he held a medium sized package. "It was a delivery," he said, his voice full of relief. Bridget realized her plan had both men nervous, and worried.

She'd pulled them into her ring of danger, and she couldn't be any more remorseful for having done so.

After a few more knocks at the door, and Doc Walker needing to attend to patients, it seemed like Hugo wouldn't turn up. Perhaps he'd sensed he was walking into a trap. Except Bridget didn't believe he was intelligent enough to work it out for himself.

Morning came and went, with no Hugo in sight. The three shared a light lunch that Hilda Walker had prepared for them. Bridget had cleaned up the kitchen and returned to her position in the infirmary, when there was yet another knock at the door.

This time Wyatt left the room to answer the door. Bridget held her breath. As much as she knew Hugo could be brutal, he could also come across as a respectable man when he wanted.

Chapter Twenty-One

Wyatt wore a white doctor's coat, and had a stethoscope around his neck. For all intents and purposes, he was a doctor. "Good afternoon, Sir," he said as he answered the door. "What can I do for you today?" He ushered the stranger into the waiting room.

From the drawing Bridget made, Wyatt knew this was Hugo Jacobs. The man gave off bad vibes, which put Wyatt on edge.

The man reached into a pocket inside his jacket, and Wyatt stiffened. Was he reaching for a gun?

"I'm here about the woman with amnesia," he said matter-of-factly as he continued to search his pockets. "She is my wife." He finally found what he was looking for, and handed over the train tickets.

Wyatt glanced down at them. "Mr. Hugo Jacobs, Mrs. Bridget Jacobs," Wyatt said, reading from the tickets. "Follow me," he said. "Simply seeing a loved one can often trigger a memory," Wyatt said, reciting the information Doc Walker had given him.

He watched as the other man trembled. The realization his *wife* might remember while in front of witnesses seemed to worry him. Wyatt was on high alert. He wore his holster under the white jacket and out of sight. It was reassuring.

He'd signaled the deputies as he'd closed the front door, leaving it unlocked. "Through this door and to your left," Wyatt instructed.

He knew the exact moment Jacobs spotted Bridget. He sprinted toward her, his arms outstretched. "Hold up their pardner," Wyatt told the kidnapper. "Your wife is fragile. You are likely to scare her. Take it easy." He again repeated the words told to him by the real doctor.

Hugo stopped in his tracks. "I wouldn't want to do that," he said quietly. It sounded as though he actually cared. The criminal put on a good show, Wyatt had to give him that.

Wyatt wanted to take him down right away, but had to be patient. He needed to witness first hand, Hugo claiming Bridget as his wife. His heart thudded and his entire body shook. Wyatt knew he needed to get himself under control or he would ruin this entire ruse.

He had done this sort of thing many times before, and never had this reaction. Then again, he wasn't in love with the woman who had set herself up as bait.

Wyatt realized he'd admitted to himself, what he should have told Bridget from the moment he'd come to the realization he loved his make-believe wife.

"Bridget," Hugo said softly. "You look terrible, my darling." His face softened as though he really cared. All he cared about, Wyatt knew, was the inheritance Bridget brought to her marriage.

She lifted her head and stared at the man standing in front of her. "Do I know you?" she asked, her eyes piercing him.

"My darling, I'm your husband. Don't you remember?" He briefly faced Wyatt, then turned back to Bridget. "Ask the doctor – I gave him the proof you're my wife."

Bridget's lips quivered upwards. Then she stood. "You are no more my husband, than Wyatt is a doctor!" she snarled.

Wyatt stepped forward and held the man by the arms. The two deputies rushed into the room and took over. "Hugo Jacobs," Deputy Simpson said, "You are under arrest for kidnap, torture, and attempted fraud." He placed the man in handcuffs and prepared to walk him out.

"Wait," Hugo said. "But…I…" Hugo glared at Bridget as though this was all her fault. "There's proof," he spluttered as he was taken away.

Bridget stood then, and came to stand in front of him. "No Hugo, there is no proof because we are not married." She turned to Wyatt then back to Hugo. "Wyatt and I are married," she said. Hugo's jaw dropped, as she knew it would. She then waved for the deputies to take him away. Out of her sight. Unfortunately, it wasn't the last time she would see him. There would have to be a trial.

At least now he was captured, Bridget didn't have to worry about Hugo pursuing her again.

She stepped into Wyatt's arms, and they stood together for what seemed forever. "Thank you," Bridget told her husband, her eyes filled with tears.

He kissed her forehead, then whispered. "I would do anything for you, including laying down my life." He paused for a moment, deciding whether he should tell her the truth. In Wyatt's mind, the time was right. "There's something I have to tell you," he whispered. Bridget stared up at him, anticipation written all over her face. "I love you Bridget Hawkins, and never want to lose you."

She continued to stare at him, her tears now overflowing. "I love you, too, Wyatt. I was sure you wanted an annulment when this was all over."

Instead of answering, Wyatt leaned down and kissed her lips. He knew it wouldn't be for the last time.

~*~

Wyatt reluctantly stepped into the sheriff's office. Given a choice he would stay with Bridget. She was still shaken, which was not surprising, but insisted he would do whatever was required. He had a job to do, and Bridget urged him to do it. He had already requested a judge for Jacobs' trial, and now waited for a response. There was a ton of paperwork to be done – Wyatt's least favorite part of his job.

The one thing he did avoid doing, was visit Jacobs in the cells. Wyatt was a professional. He'd been sheriff for most of his adult life, and knew how to control his temper. In this case, Wyatt didn't trust himself. "I'll come with you, if it helps," Deputy Simpson told him.

Wyatt was about to deny the suggestion, but decided to take up his offer after all. If for no other reason but to reassure himself the criminal was behind bars. With his sheriff's badge pinned to his shirt, Wyatt stepped into the cells. Deputy Simpson was right behind him.

He'd rehearsed a speech in his mind. Wyatt planned to tell Hugo Jacobs what he'd done to Bridget. How he'd almost killed her, and ruined her life. He stood in front of the locked cell, opening his mouth to speak.

Instead, he stared at the would-be killer. Hugo stared back.

"You can't do this!" Hugo Jacobs complained.

Wyatt couldn't help but laugh. Not the sort of laugh you'd have when something was funny, but a dry, unbelieving laugh. If nothing else, it reinforced to Wyatt the man in the cell truly was insane. He would ask Doc Walker to do an assessment before the trial began.

"I've contacted the judge about your trial, and will provide details when I have them," Wyatt said, then turned to leave.

"Wait!" Hugo called. He studied Wyatt again. "I thought you were a doctor," he said glaring at the sheriff's badge.

"And I thought you were a man," the sheriff told him, then left Hugo to his own thoughts.

Back at his desk, Wyatt couldn't concentrate. "I'm taking the rest of the day off," he told the deputies. "Thank you for your help today."

"Of course," Deputy Simpson said.

"Anything for you and the missus," Deputy Hartwick added.

Wyatt couldn't have asked for better deputies. They carried out their work in a professional manner, and were always there when he needed them.

Pushing his chair back, Wyatt stood. He glanced around the room. His heart was heavy, as though this was the last time he would enter the sheriff's office. He'd had no such plans, so Wyatt was unsure why he felt that way now.

Perhaps because his make-believe wife had become his real wife, and his life would never be the same again.

Chapter Twenty-Two

Bridget sat nervously next to Wyatt as the trial began. They were both required to give evidence, and it made Bridget uneasy.

Hugo stood at the podium to the side of the room. The two deputies stood either side of their prisoner. The judge sat a table not far away, and glanced around the room.

In a few days, it would be Christmas. For everyone's sake, Bridget hoped the trial would be heard and resolved today. She needed to prepare for Christmas Day, and didn't need the distraction.

Truthfully though, she wanted the trial over so they could enjoy Christmas, but it was doubtful it would happen. No matter, she couldn't see how Hugo could be found not guilty.

Judge Anthony MacArthur lifted the gavel and pounded it. "The court will be in order," he shouted over the murmurings of those in attendance. Silence prevailed.

Deputy Simpson read out the list of charges, then handed the list to the judge. Bridget was called to the witness stand, her eyes on Wyatt the entire time. Every now and then, Judge MacArthur grunted. He interrupted once or twice to clarify something Bridget had said, and she expanded on her answer. When she felt as though she could no longer handle the interrogation, she glanced at Wyatt who nodded his reassurance. She could do this.

She had to do it, or risk Hugo being set free again.

"I believe you jumped from a moving train to escape the accused," Judge MacArthur said.

"Yes, Your Honor, I did." Even to her own ears, Bridget's voice was full of emotion. She wasn't sure she could continue, but knew she must.

"You may step down, Mrs. Hawkins."

Bridget almost cried with relief.

Wyatt rushed across the room and helped Bridget down the few steps. He escorted her back to her seat.

"Sheriff, I'll hear from you now," the judge said, and Wyatt took the stand. "I believe you witnessed the victim leaping from the train."

"I did Your Honor. It was the first time I'd seen such a thing. I knew immediately Miss Spencer had to be desperate." He glanced across at Bridget before continuing. "She sustained several injuries in the fall. I took her to Doc Walker, and he patched her up." Wyatt had given evidence before, and Bridget wished she possessed the same state of calm he did. He told the judge how they'd set the accused up, with him pretending he was a doctor, and Bridget pretending she had amnesia. He described how the prisoner was finally arrested.

"It's all lies," Hugo shouted.

The judge grunted again. "If the prisoner cannot keep quiet, he is to be returned to the cells." Judge MacArthur slammed the gavel again.

Hugo cringed and kept his mouth shut after the judge's threat.

After Wyatt, Doc Walker was called to the stand. He testified about Bridget's injuries, and her ongoing treatment. He explained how she came to be so thin, as well as sleep deprived.

"I also assessed the accused," Doc Walker said. "In my opinion, the accused is not insane. Hugo Jacobs put on a good show, trying to prove he is insane, but nothing pointed to that diagnosis."

Typical Hugo, thinking he was better off in an insane asylum than jail. He might think that was the case, but from what Bridget had learned, it was far from the truth.

After his extensive testimony, Doc Walker was excused from the witness box and returned to his seat.

"All stand," Deputy Simpson called, and the judge left the room. "Proceedings will continue in two hours," the deputy announced. The prisoner was taken back to the cells.

Bridget breathed a sigh of relief. The main part of the trial was over. After he'd eaten, Judge MacArthur would read through all his notes and the documentation he'd been provided.

She hoped when the court resumed, he would announce his conclusion. Except there was no guarantee it would happen.

~*~

"All rise," Deputy Simpson announced, and the judge reentered the room. "Be seated," he said, then went back to stand beside the accused.

Judge MacArthur fiddled with the papers on his desk. He pulled a notepad closer to himself and began to read aloud. The judge went through the sequence of events that led to Bridget's abduction and subsequent torture. The fact Hugo knew about her inheritance, although it had not been discovered how he found out. He also mentioned Hugo's penchant for lying to get whatever he wanted. "That includes," he said gravely, "Lying about the fact he was Miss Spencer's husband. And he had the audacity to do so on the railway line the victim happened to own."

Bridget studied the judge. He'd done his homework.

"He starved her, and tortured her with sleep deprivation." The judge glanced across at Bridget. "I believe his plan was to make her compliant to marry him, then dispose of his new wife."

She was suddenly aware of Wyatt's eyes on her. He knew she had an inheritance, but he had no idea how much it was, or how rich her family had been.

He reached across and held her hand. Was the judge almost ready to make his judgement? She hoped so. The day had been incredibly stressful.

"Hugo Jacobs, I find you guilty on all counts," the judge told Hugo. "I have grave concerns about public safety, should you ever be freed. Therefore, I sentence you to hanging by the neck until you are dead." Judge MacArthur slammed down the gavel, stood, then left the room.

Bridget sat motionless. All along she'd been concerned the judge would sentence Hugo to only a small number of years, but thankfully, had been proven wrong.

She glanced up to Hugo's pale face. As he was removed from the courthouse, he glanced back at her. Not an ounce of regret or apology in his expression.

As much as Hugo deserved the sentence he received, Bridget felt sorry for him. Wyatt put an arm around her, and led Bridget out of the makeshift court room.

Evil had been captured and punished. It was the best outcome she could have hoped for.

~*~

Christmas Day, when it finally came around was quiet for the pair. Although they were invited to join Doc and Hilda Walker for the day, they refused. Opting instead to spend the time together, just the two of them.

It was their first Christmas together as husband and wife, and knew it wouldn't be their last. Bridget thought of Hugo sitting in his jail cell, but only for a moment. Everything Hugo got, Hugo deserved.

Early in the new year, Hugo would be transported to the state prison where he would be hanged. In the meantime, he sat alone in the cells behind the sheriff's office. Exactly where he belonged.

Bridget had endured a lot of suffering because of Hugo's greed. She knew he was bad news from the start. It was the reason she had always deflected from him. Sadly, Father hadn't seen his intent the way Bridget had. Father saw the good in everyone. He believed Hugo would make a wonderful husband for his only child.

He couldn't have been more wrong.

Thinking of her parents made Bridget melancholy. She owed them a great deal. Without them, where would she be now?

She stared down at the festively decorated table. Both she and Wyatt had planned and baked the past two days to ensure they had a traditional Christmas dinner. They wanted it to be one to be remembered.

Despite their refusal from Doc and Hilda Walker, Hilda had gifted them a Christmas cake. "It's my way of commemorating your first Christmas," she'd said. "There are far better times ahead for the two of you," she said, then winked before walking away.

Hilda was right. Better times was what they both craved. What they didn't want to remember was the trauma Bridget had endured, along with Hugo's trial. Christmas was a time for peace and reflection, not for reliving the bad times.

"Happy Christmas," Wyatt said, then pulled Bridget to him. He leaned down and now that she was his real wife, kissed her thoroughly without having to feel guilty about it.

Bridget loved Wyatt with all her heart, and knew without Hugo kidnapping her, they would never have met.

Epilogue

Eleven months later…

Wyatt stood back, and stared. "I don't think…" He rubbed a hand across his chin. "It's not straight." He stepped forward and straightened the painting that sat in the entrance hall. The new Inn was almost ready to open.

It was top of their list. A place where visitors to town could stay. Decent people didn't want to stay in the saloon.

It had been a real dilemma when Bridget arrived, and she didn't want to see anyone else put in the same situation. Although in her case it worked out for the best.

Bridget's inheritance was far greater than Wyatt had ever imagined. When the money arrived in his bank account, they sat down and etched out a plan. For Bridget, the most important thing was for most of the money to go to charity. That was her desire, and always had been.

A large donation was made to the church and the ladies auxiliary, with the stipulation the money was to be distributed to those in need. Bridget insisted on an ongoing donation. How else would they use all that money?

They'd also planned for a school, as well as a teacher. The way things stood now, there was no school. All children needed an education – no matter how rich or how poor they were.

The Spencer Family mansion in Helena was far too big, besides, neither of them wanted to leave Halliwell Junction. It was home to them both. Instead of selling it, or leaving Bridget's former home sitting empty, it was renovated, and turned into a refuge for women. Before her encounter with Hugo, Bridget had no idea violence against women existed. Her eyes had been opened to the aggression many women endured.

Last on their list, but by no means least, was a home they would live in. Wyatt's dream was always to retire to a small ranch. A place where he could bring up his children, and live a peaceful existence with his wife.

They found the perfect place about thirty minutes drive outside of town. It needed a little work, and Wyatt had reveled in fixing the ranch up to suit their needs.

"I can't believe the Inn is almost ready to open," Bridget told Wyatt. "It has been a lot of work, I know, but it's desperately needed," she added. All profits from the Inn would go to charity. Wherever it was needed, it would be distributed. Locals had been employed to build it, and locals had been employed to run it.

Wyatt nodded. His arms went around his much loved wife. As she held their two-month-old son, he glanced down into the baby's face. "My heart has never been so full," he whispered.

Bridget loved everything about this man, her husband.

Already, in their second year of marriage, they'd achieved so much. Without her father's tireless hard work, and good business sense, it would never have happened. Bridget knew she was blessed.

She liked to think her parents were looking down on her little family, pleased to know Bridget had found the man of her heart. She hoped too, they saw their sweet grandson.

Her wish for baby Joseph was to grow up kind, generous, and loving, just like his father.

From the Author

Thank you so much for reading my book – I hope you enjoyed it.

I would greatly appreciate you leaving a review where you purchased, even if it is only a one-liner. It helps to have my books more visible!

~*~

About the Author

Multi-published, award-winning and bestselling author Cheryl Wright, former secretary, debt collector, account manager, writing coach, and shopping tour hostess, loves reading.

She writes historical romantic suspense and historical western romance.

She lives in Melbourne, Australia, and is married with two adult children and has six grandchildren, and twin great-grandchildren.

When she's not writing, she can be found in her craft room making greeting cards.

Links

Website: *http://www.cheryl-wright.com/*

Facebook Reader Group:
https://www.facebook.com/groups/cherylwrightauthor/

Join My Newsletter:

https://cheryl-wright.com/newsletter/
(and receive a free book)